A FEAR OF VENGEANCE

Detective Inspector Bill Forward is working at Hackney police station when he and a police constable answer a 999 call from a woman in distress. When they arrest the woman's husband, whose brutal attack has left her with terrible injuries, DI Forward considers the case closed . . . but he is wrong. Having served his prison sentence, the sadistic Bob Plummer is hell-bent on revenge. After attacking the police constable who assisted in his arrest, Plummer goes looking for DI Forward. It is only a matter of time before he strikes again. The question is: will DI Forward be ready?

Books by Ray Alan
Published by The House of Ulverscroft:

A GAME OF MURDER

RAY ALAN

♦

A FEAR OF VENGEANCE

Complete and Unabridged

ULVERSCROFT
Leicester

First published in Great Britain in 2010 by
Robert Hale Limited
London

First Large Print Edition
published 2011
by arrangement with
Robert Hale Limited
London

British Library CIP Data

Alan, Ray.
  A fear of vengeance.
  1. Wife abuse- -Fiction. 2. Ex-convicts- -Fiction.
  3. Revenge- -Fiction. 4. Detective and mystery stories.
  5. Large type books.
  I. Title
  823.9'2–dc22

  ISBN 978–1–44480–516–1

Published by
F. A. Thorpe (Publishing)
Anstey, Leicestershire

Set by Words & Graphics Ltd.
Anstey, Leicestershire
Printed and bound in Great Britain by
T. J. International Ltd., Padstow, Cornwall

This book is printed on acid-free paper

1

Detective Inspector Bill Forward was enjoying his Saturday morning in bed. It was the first time in weeks that he had no case to worry about and was able to relax. His wife, Jane, knew that he had been disturbed by his last case because he seldom mentioned it. She made her way to the bedroom with a tray of tea and after pouring out two cups, put one on the bedside table beside him and got back into bed herself.

He opened one eye and looked at the alarm clock. 'I can't believe it's after half past seven and I'm still in bed.' He smiled.

'Well, at the rate you have been working these past few weeks, you deserve it. But you mustn't overdo it, Bill. Any time you want to discuss anything, you know I'm a good listener. I may not be in your job but I like to help you if I can.'

'I know that, love.'

'Sit up and drink your tea. Then you can snuggle down again.'

He sat up and started to drink and she could see by the expression on his face that he was thinking of something unpleasant.

'How can a man be cruel to a child? I mean, to beat a six-year-old and cause her such pain, a man has to be sick,' he said.

'Well, thanks to you he's been charged and will go to court, won't he?'

'Not for another three months.'

'But your evidence will help to convict him, surely?'

'Oh yes. But at the end he will probably be given a light sentence because his defence barrister will convince the jury that he needs psychiatric help. Men like him want putting to sleep.' He sighed and said, 'If you had seen that child when Marsh and I found her you would have cried.'

'Well, try not to dwell on it too much. Think about your day off and what we can do today. You get your head down and relax while I have a shower.'

Bill smiled and did just that. With his head on the pillow, he closed his eyes and drifted off to sleep again. Jane finished her shower and went quietly to the bedroom, managing to dress without disturbing him. It was an hour later when Bill woke up. When he saw the time he got out of bed and went to the bathroom to get washed. He shaved and took his morning shower and soon felt more relaxed. The case he had been working on was one that had taken all his patience and skill to bring to a satisfactory conclusion and he kept thinking about it. He had always wondered why a man would want to abuse a child. The details of this case had sickened even this very experienced policeman and he looked forward to giving evidence against the man once he was finally brought to court. He now hoped nothing else would come along to spoil his well-earned weekend at home.

His wife was downstairs, about to prepare his favourite cooked breakfast of bacon, eggs and mushrooms when the phone rang. She picked up the receiver and heard the voice of a young man.

'Hello. Is that Mrs Forward?'

'Yes.'

'It's Terry Kennedy, Mrs Forward. Is Mr Forward there? I've got some information I think he'll want to know about. If he wants to call me back I'm at my aunt's. He knows the number.'

'He's in the shower at the moment, Terry. Aren't you one of the boys at Father O'Connor's youth club?'

'Yes, that's right.'

'Is it very urgent or can I give him his breakfast first?'

'Oh, let him have his breakfast. Sorry to have disturbed you — only I promised I'd let him know if anything like this happened.'

'I'll tell him as soon as he's eaten.'

'Thank you, Mrs Forward.'

Jane replaced the receiver and was tempted to tell her husband straightaway but decided that today he should relax and have a proper breakfast. At that moment she heard the bathroom door open and called up, 'Would you like me to put the bacon on?'

'I'd rather you put a dress on,' he replied. 'But if it's all you've got to wear I suppose you'll have to. I'll be there in two minutes, my love.'

Smiling at his remark, Jane was happy that he was more like himself again. She got his favourite breakfast started and hoped that whatever Terry Kennedy wanted to tell him wouldn't spoil their weekend together.

★   ★   ★

Bob Plummer had just been released from serving his time and was on his way to a boarding house. He had no home to go to as his wife had divorced him and given up the flat they had rented.

He had been his own worst enemy, due to a violent temper that he had never been able to control. A temper that had made a neighbour call the police when she heard his wife scream for help. It had taken two policemen to arrest him and had left his wife with terrible injuries to her face. But during his time in prison he had made a promise to himself that once free, he would wreak vengeance on those police officers responsible for his incarceration. All he could think about was the pleasure of making them suffer.

★　★　★

Bill had finished breakfast and gave Jane a contented smile. 'Thank you, my love. That was delicious. Another cup of coffee and I'll be ready for anything.' Jane was used to his love of coffee and had made sure there was plenty in the cafetière. She waited until he had finished and was sitting in a comfortable armchair before she told him of Terry's phone call.

'He didn't say what it was that he wanted to tell me?'

'No. Only that he thought you would want to know. He's at his aunt's. He said you've got the number.'

'Yes. Could you get my diary? It's in my jacket.'

Jane went to his jacket in the hall and took the diary to him. 'Is he the boy whose father you arrested?'

'Yes, his father got fifteen years but he died

5

in prison. His mother didn't want her son to grow up like him and before she died I promised to keep an eye on the boy. Father O'Connor took him under his wing and got him into his boys' club. He's turned out to be a good lad. The boys don't have to be Catholic to be helped by Father O'Connor.' He dialled the number of Terry's aunt and it was Terry that answered. 'Hello, lad. It's Inspector Forward. I hear you wanted me.'

'Yes, Mr Forward. I think that Ronnie Hicks, one of the boys at the club, has started on drugs. A man came the other night when Father O'Connor wasn't here, and was trying to get us all interested. I think he was a pusher.'

'This man, have you seen him before?'

'Yes. He was hanging around about a week ago.'

'Have you spoken to Ronnie about it?'

'No. I didn't think I should get involved. That's why I called you.'

'You did right. Why do you think Ronnie is taking drugs?'

'I went to the toilet and while I was washing my hands I saw him in the mirror, sniffing some powder from the back of his hand. It'll be cocaine, won't it?'

'Sounds like it. And you haven't noticed him doing this before?'

'No. And I don't think he knew I saw him last night in the toilet either. Otherwise he'd have said something, wouldn't he?'

Bill was thoughtful. 'Yes. What sort of boy is this Ronnie Hicks? Friendly?'

'I've always got on with him. He's not what you'd call a troublemaker,' said Terry. 'But if that pusher has got him on drugs he wants stopping before he goes on to something stronger.'

'Let me think about this. Keep an eye on him but don't let anyone know you called me. These drug dealers are not very nice people.'

'I know. Don't worry — I'll only call you from the house.'

'Good lad. I'll be in touch.' Bill put the receiver down and, after giving it some consideration, decided to call his friend Dave Norris in the drugs squad and get his advice. He was about to phone when his mobile rang. He saw that the caller was Marsh, his sergeant, and wondered what had prompted the call. Hoping that it was nothing serious, he answered.

'Good morning, sunshine. Now, before you say anything, I have just eaten a lovely breakfast and I don't want to spoil it by getting indigestion. So I hope your call isn't to tell me a new case has just come in that will ruin my weekend.'

'No, sir. I just wondered if Baa-Baa had been in touch. Only he called me from home to check your mobile number.'

'Baa-Baa! Is that how the lower ranks are referring to our esteemed Superintendent Lamb? Be careful, Sergeant, or he'll put you on transfer and I don't want to lose you now that you're almost a proper detective.'

Marsh smiled to himself. 'Thank you, sir. I just wondered what he wanted, that's all.'

'As soon as I know I shall tell you. But till then I shall try and relax again. Goodbye, Sergeant.' Bill rang off, trying to think what his super could want him for. He then rang Inspector Dave Norris and left a message on his voicemail, before sitting back to read the morning paper. He was just getting interested in an article when his mobile rang and he saw that the caller was Superintendent Lamb.

'Good morning, sir,' said Bill, wondering again what he wanted.

'Sorry to bother you on your day off, Forward. Only I've had a call from my colleague at Hackney about a man you arrested when you were a sergeant there. His name was Bob Plummer. Do you remember him?'

'I certainly do — he's a nasty bit of work. We had a 999 call and when we got to the flat we could hear screaming. We forced our way in and it took two of us to restrain and cuff him. He'd beaten his wife so badly she needed plastic surgery before she could show her face again. The judge gave him five years for GBH with intent.'

'I hear he threatened you when he was sentenced.'

'Oh yes, the usual, 'I'll get even with you two,' and a few choice words suggesting our parents weren't married. You know the sort of thing. What about him?'

'He was released on Tuesday and yesterday the officer who was with you when you arrested him, a Sergeant Lockhart, was badly beaten up.'

Bill became concerned and asked, 'How badly?'

'Facial bruising, three broken ribs and some front teeth, apparently,' said Lamb.

'And Plummer did this?' Bill asked.

'The sergeant only got a glimpse of him before he went down and lost consciousness but he was sure it was him.'

'So he made it to sergeant. I'm glad. He was a nice chap.'

Lamb sounded awkward as he said, 'They put out an APB to have Plummer picked up but so far there's no sign of him. He seems to be lying low somewhere and that gives me a problem.'

'What's that, sir?'

'He told Lockhart that he would sort you out as well. With this man on the loose, I can't afford to take chances. I've arranged for an armed protection officer to give you twenty-four-hour protection until Plummer is caught and back in custody.'

Bill got up from his chair and closed the door, afraid that Jane might hear his conversation. 'Is that really necessary, sir?'

'The men under me are my responsibility, Forward.'

'Yes, I know that, sir. But I . . . '

'I've made my decision and that's all there is to it. I've put PC Roberts on to start with. You know him, so if you see him keeping an eye on your house or hanging around the nick, you'll know what he's doing. I'm sending Marsh round with a panic button so that you can call Roberts if there's an emergency. Hopefully it won't be for long but keep your eyes open. Now try and relax and enjoy the weekend off. And that's an order.'

'I will. Thank you, sir,' said Bill, with a hint of sarcasm. After he rang off, Jane opened the door and saw him put his mobile down.

'Were you on a call? Sorry,' she said.

'It's all right, love, it's nothing important. I was just going to call Dave Norris and tell him what Terry Kennedy said, about a drug pusher hanging around the club. And I thought I might get Marsh over here and tell him what's going on.'

'Yes, why don't you?' Jane smiled. 'He could stay for lunch if you would like him to.'

'We'll see. He might have other arrangements if WPC Hamilton is off duty. And I know where he'd rather be if she is.' He grinned.

Jane left the room and Bill wondered whether to tell her about the armed protection officer he'd had forced on him. But he decided not to worry her and hoped Plummer would be in custody before he could be a threat. He picked up his mobile and called Marsh quickly to tell him not to say anything about the panic button in front of Jane. Then he thought about the ridiculous situation he was in and the words of a song from a Gilbert and Sullivan operetta came to mind: 'A policeman's lot is not a happy one.'

2

Dave Norris returned Bill's call, and when he heard about Ronnie Hicks and the man seen hanging around the club, he was anxious to meet Terry Kennedy.

'Where can I find this Terry?' Dave asked.

'I don't think it would be safe for you to go to the club or where he's living. You might be seen and recognized.'

'So where do you suggest?'

'My office would be safe,' said Bill. 'He'd get the bus and walk round the back through the car park. He knows that way and nobody would see him going into the nick from there.'

Dave looked at his watch. 'Could he be there just after lunchtime?'

'I'll ring him and arrange it.'

'Good. I'll get him to look at some mugshots of known dealers and see if he recognizes the man he saw at the boys' club.'

'Good idea. Terry's a nice lad and you can trust him. He'll do anything he can to help. Let me know how you get on.'

'I will. Cheers, Bill.'

As soon as they had finished their

12

conversation, Bill rang Terry and told him what he had arranged. A few moments later the front doorbell rang and Bill quickly went to the window and saw that Marsh had arrived. 'It's Marsh. I'll get it,' he called to Jane, then went to the hall and opened the door. As Marsh walked in Bill saw PC Roberts sitting in a car almost opposite and realized how serious his superior thought Bob Plummer's threat might be. As soon as they were alone, Marsh gave him two small packets.

'Here are the panic buttons,' Marsh said quietly. 'There's one for your wife as well, just in case she needs it.'

'Did Lamb tell you what this is all about?' asked Bill.

'Yes. And I noticed you've got Roberts outside keeping an eye on the place in case Plummer turns up. What do these panic buttons look like?'

Bill unwrapped one to show him. 'They're similar to those worn by elderly people if they fall or need assistance.'

'Do you have to wear it round your neck?'

'Round your neck or in your pocket, it doesn't matter as long as you can get at it quickly.'

'This Plummer sounds a right villain. Let's hope they pick him up before he finds out where you are,' said Marsh.

'How nice to know you care about me. I feel quite emotional now,' Bill mocked, wiping a tear from his eye.

Marsh threw an upward glance of despair. 'I happen to be serious. Keep that panic button with you just in case.'

'Yes, Sergeant. Now I'm being serious. My wife wanted to know if you would like to stay for some lunch.'

'That's very kind but I'll have to get back to the office. I've arranged to meet someone. But please thank her for me.'

'I will. And thank you for coming. Keep in touch and I'll see you at the office on Monday.'

When Marsh had gone, Bill told Jane that his sergeant had another lunch date. He then sat looking at the panic button and realized the dangerous situation he could be in if Bob Plummer wasn't caught soon and was able to carry out his threat on the policeman he knew at Hackney as Sergeant Forward.

★　★　★

Dave Norris finished his lunch and went to Bill's office to meet Terry Kennedy, as arranged. He knocked and opened the door, surprised to see Marsh standing there, smiling, as if expecting him.

'Oh, hello, sir. I thought you were someone else,' said Marsh, losing his smile.

'It was obvious by your beaming face that it wasn't me you were expecting, Sergeant,' Dave grinned.

'I'm afraid Inspector Forward won't be in today, sir.'

'I know. I was speaking to him earlier. He kindly arranged for me to meet a young lad here who might have a lead for me on a drug pusher.'

'Oh, right. I'll leave you to it then. I'm meeting a colleague for a late lunch.' At that moment there was a knock on the door and Marsh opened it to see Terry Kennedy there with WPC Sally Hamilton standing just behind him. 'Come in, Terry. Inspector Norris is expecting you.'

As Terry was ushered in, Dave smiled and said, 'Looks like both our dates have arrived. Have a good lunch.'

Marsh returned his smile and said, 'Thank you, sir,' and as he and Sally walked away, Dave closed the door.

'I'm Inspector Norris. Come and sit down, Terry.' He smiled and indicated a chair near Bill's desk. As Terry sat, Dave pulled up another chair for himself. 'Thank you for coming, Terry. Inspector Forward tells me

15

you might have seen the man that was pushing drugs on the boys at your club.'

Terry went over the events, including his being convinced that Ronnie Hicks was sniffing what looked like cocaine. Dave listened with interest.

'Had you seen this man hanging about the club before?'

'I might have but I can't be sure. There are various people around from time to time. It just so happens I remember this man. He looked a bit tasty.'

'By tasty you mean like a man who could be threatening?'

'Yes. I wouldn't like to cross him.'

Dave was thoughtful for a moment and then opened a file of photographs. 'I want you to look at these mugshots and see if you recognize any of them. Take your time.'

Terry went carefully through the photographs and stopped at one. 'This is the man who came to the club.'

Dave looked at the face of a well-built man in his late forties. 'Benny Sutherland. He was inside until recently. So he's out and about again, is he? Well, you're right about him being tasty. He's a drug pusher and a very nasty one too.'

Dave decided to be frank. 'If this man does appear again and Ronnie keeps getting supplied with drugs, would you mind carrying a wire and talking to Ronnie so that we can hear what he says to you?'

Terry was excited by the thought and said, 'You mean have a hidden microphone on me?'

Dave smiled and said, 'Yes.'

'I'd like that, as long as you show me how to work it.'

'Don't worry. It just clips into your pocket like an innocent-looking pen, and all you have to do is switch it on. It's very simple. Would you agree to that?'

'Yes, sir. I hate drugs. I've seen what they do to people. So if I can stop the boys at our club getting hooked I'm all for it.'

'Ronnie is at the club most nights, is he?'

'Yes.'

'I'll make arrangements and we can take it from there. But I must warn you that if anyone knows you're wired you could be in danger and I don't want you getting into trouble so not a word to anyone about this. The only other person who will know is Inspector Forward, understood?'

'Yes, sir. And don't worry. I won't do anything stupid.'

Dave got up and shook Terry's hand. 'Thanks for coming. I'll be in touch.'

Terry watched him leave the office and

then went out the same way he came in, through the car park. As he caught the bus home, he felt proud that he was going to be trusted to do something so important.

★ ★ ★

As soon as Dave Norris got back to his own office, he rang Bill Forward.

'Hello, Bill. It's Dave. I thought you'd like to know that I've just seen Terry Kennedy.'

'How did you get on with him?'

'He's a nice young man and we got on fine. He recognized the mugshot of a pusher with form and agreed to be wired and talk to the Hicks boy. We might learn a bit more about his supplier that way,' said Dave.

Bill became worried as he said, 'I don't want Terry put in any danger. What happens if something goes wrong and it's known that he's wired?'

'Don't worry, Bill. All he will have is an ordinary-looking biro and he will have full control with a simple switch.'

'I hope you're right.'

'Terry wants to do this, Bill. The boy is really keen to help. He'll be fine, so stop worrying.'

'It's just that I feel responsible for him. Keep in touch and let me know how it goes.'

'I will.'

Bill put the phone down and tried to get back to reading the newspaper. But he kept thinking about Terry getting involved and hoped he wouldn't be in any danger. Then he thought about the armed policeman outside the house and became uncomfortable. Bill had joined the force when the English police seldom carried a firearm. Now they were becoming more and more common and Bill wished they weren't. He was sad that the old days of policing as he knew it were gone and unlikely to ever come back.

★ ★ ★

Sergeant Marsh enjoyed his lunch with Sally Hamilton and was pleased with her news of promotion.

'So, does this mean I will no longer be your superior and able to boss you about, Sergeant?' Marsh asked jokingly.

Grinning proudly she said, 'I'm afraid so, Sergeant.'

Satisfied no-one was looking, he kissed her cheek and said quietly, 'Congratulations. When do you get your stripes?'

'Why? Do you want to sew them on for me?'

Marsh laughed. 'You wouldn't ask that if

you saw me with a needle. But seriously, DI Forward will be glad you got promotion. I know he recommended you for it.'

'He's nice, your boss.'

'Yes, he is. And his wife's nice too. I just hope they don't get a visit from a certain Bob Plummer.'

'Who's he?'

'He's a thug that my governor and another officer arrested for wife-beating. He got out of prison a couple of days ago. He went and beat up the officer and threatened to do the same to Sergeant Forward.'

'So he's got a vengeance syndrome. How long was his sentence?'

'His wife needed plastic surgery so he got five years but had the usual time off for good behaviour.'

'And he's carried a grudge all this time!'

'Yes, apparently so.'

'He sounds dangerous. Where is he now? Broadmoor?'

'I wish he was. There's an APB out for him but so far he's not been seen.'

'You're joking!'

'No, I'm not. The super's given my boss a twenty-four-hour armed protection officer until Plummer's picked up. I wish I could do something. I feel useless not being able to help.'

20

'Who's the armed protection officer?'

'It's PC Roberts at the moment. I don't know who's taking over from him,' said Marsh.

Sally reached out and took his hand. 'Don't worry. They may have Plummer back in custody soon.'

'I hope so,' Marsh sighed. 'I really do. The governor must be fed up, not able to go out without an armed nursemaid to keep an eye on him. And he's worried about his wife too.'

'Does she know about Plummer's threat?' asked Sally.

'He hadn't told her when I was there earlier. Didn't want to worry her, he said.'

Sally glanced at the wall clock. 'Look at the time. I'll have to get back. Will you come round later?'

He smiled. 'Of course I will.'

She blew him a kiss and walked from the canteen. Sally knew he was worried about his boss and hoped that the Bob Plummer saga would soon be over, for all their sakes.

★   ★   ★

Father O'Connor had phoned the police station and was told that Inspector Forward would not be there until Monday. Being anxious to talk to him, he called his home

21

number and Jane answered.

'It's Father O'Connor, Mrs Forward.'

'Hello, Father. No doubt it's my husband you want.'

'Yes, if it's convenient.'

'I'll call him. Bill. It's Father O'Connor on the line.'

Bill picked up the extension. 'Hello, Father.'

'Sorry to bother you at home but I think you should know that one or two of the boys have seen a man hanging around the club lately. He's been there again this lunchtime and unless my judgement of character is very much mistaken, he's up to no good.'

'And the boys have seen the same man before?'

'Yes. Three of them have been approached by him during the past week. He's been telling them he can get things to make them feel good, much cheaper than anyone else. Now what does that suggest to you, Inspector?'

'The first thing that comes to mind is drugs.'

'That's exactly what I thought. And I don't want my lads succumbing to temptation of that sort.'

'Have you spoken to them on that subject?'

'I thought I would wait until I'd spoken to you.'

22

'Are you at the club now?'

'Yes.'

'I'll get Sergeant Marsh to come and show you a photo of the man I think it might be. Will you be there for a while?'

'Yes.'

'Good. I'll get him there as soon as I can. Then we can decide on what to do. Meantime, say nothing to the boys.'

'I understand. Thank you, Inspector.'

Bill ended his call and immediately phoned Marsh. 'It's me. Get the mugshots of drug pushers and take them over to Father O'Connor at the club. Then let me know if he recognizes anyone. It seems Benny Sutherland or his pals are leaning on some of the lads. If they are, Dave Norris will want to know.'

'I'll get over there right away. Does it matter if any of the boys recognize me as a copper?' asked Marsh.

'If they do, just be friendly as though it's a social call to Father O'Connor and not police business.'

'Right, I'm on my way.'

Bill rang off, still worried about Terry Kennedy getting wired and involved. It wasn't often that Bill got worried but this time he was. He had a nasty gut feeling that Terry could be walking into danger.

3

It was just gone 4 p.m. when Marsh got back into his car and phoned Bill Forward.

'Hello, sir. Father O'Connor confirmed that Benny was the man. Do you want me to go back to the office or come over to you?'

'Come over here. I'll call Dave Norris and let him know what's happened.'

'OK. I'll see you soon.'

Bill hung up and dialled Dave's direct line and as soon as he answered, filled him in with what had happened.

'So the Father picked out Benny Sutherland too. I think we should get them both wired, Terry and the priest. Benny and his pals would never dream that the priest was wired.'

'Probably not but I don't like the idea of putting him in any danger. Upset these thugs and they don't care who they dispose of.'

'You know him well, Bill — why don't you put it to him and see what his reaction is? I don't want to waste time on this. If we can put these buggers away before they do any real harm I shall feel a lot happier. And so will you.'

As soon as Dave rang off, Bill called Father

O'Connor. 'Hello, Father. Don't mention my name in case someone hears.'

'My office door is closed so you can speak quietly and not be overheard, Bishop,' the Father said casually.

Bill smiled at being referred to as Bishop. 'I've spoken to my colleague and he wonders how you feel about being more involved in the subject we discussed?'

Lowering his voice, the Father replied, 'I will do anything I can to stop these people from spreading their evil.'

'You could put yourself in danger. You realize that?'

'I shall be going home soon and will call you from there. We can speak more freely then,' he whispered.

As Bill put the phone down, Jane came in and went to the window, careful not to be seen from outside.

'I was upstairs and noticed a man sitting in a car parked opposite. He was there earlier and seems to have been there a long time. Why do you think he's waiting there?'

Bill knew he would have to tell her. 'He's one of our chaps, love. Lamb put him there to keep an eye on us in case an unsavoury character turns up.'

Jane looked confused. 'What character?'

'A man I arrested when we were in

Hackney. He came out of prison recently and was heard to say he would look me up. He blames me for getting him put away, it seems.'

'What did he go inside for?'

'Wife-beating.'

Jane was concerned. 'So Lamb thinks this man will come looking for you? Where is he now?'

'At the moment they don't know but there's an all-ports out on him, so he's bound to turn up soon.'

'Not here, I hope,' Jane said nervously. 'So that man in the car is there in case this other man does come here?'

'Yes. But like I said, this man, Plummer, will be picked up soon, so there's no need to worry, love.' Bill gave her a reassuring smile but Jane wasn't convinced.

★　★　★

When Marsh arrived Bill asked Jane to make some tea and join them in the front room. He closed the door and lowered his voice.

'I told her about Plummer and explained that Roberts was there to keep an eye on us. But I didn't mention he was from the armed protection unit. She's nervous enough as it is.'

Marsh nodded. 'I understand, sir. Father

26

O'Connor didn't hesitate when he saw Benny Sutherland's photo. He picked him out straightaway.'

'Dave wants to have him wired. I didn't mention that just now when I phoned him at the club. It's far too easy for someone to overhear a snippet of a conversation and put two and two together. The Father's going to phone me here when he gets home then we can speak freely.'

Marsh frowned and asked, 'Do you think he would agree to being wired? I mean, him being a priest, wouldn't he think being wired was a sin?'

'That's a good point, Sergeant. But if it is considered a sin and he was wired, who would he confess to?' Bill placed a finger to his lips and opened the door with a smile. 'I heard the cups rattling. Marsh wondered if there was any of your fruit cake going spare, my love.'

She knew by the expression on Marsh's face that he had never mentioned cake. Jane put the tea tray on a table.

'Hello, Sergeant. I think there might be some left. I'll go and get it for you.'

As she left, Bill said, 'Wait till you taste her fruit cake, it's beautiful.'

Jane returned with just one slice on a plate and smiled at Marsh. 'Here we are, Sergeant.

You're in luck — that's the last slice.'

Bill's face dropped. 'You're joking.'

Jane gave Marsh a surreptitious wink, and then turned to Bill. 'You mustn't fill yourself up with cake or you won't have any appetite for our night out.'

'What night out?'

'Well, there's nothing on the television, so I was hoping we would go out for a nice meal somewhere.'

Marsh grinned. 'You were right about this cake being beautiful, sir.' Then he took another mouthful.

Bill stopped himself from saying what he wanted to and gave Marsh a half-hearted smile. 'Glad you're enjoying it.'

'So where shall we go tonight?' Jane asked Bill.

'Well, don't forget that wherever we go we'll have Roberts or whoever takes over from him keeping a beady eye on us.'

'But he won't be sitting with us, will he?' asked Jane.

'No but . . . '

'Well, there you are, so what about the Dining Room? It's not usually too busy on a Saturday.'

'That's because it's rather expensive. What about fish and chips in paper bags?' Bill asked.

Jane kept a straight face and said, 'That's

an idea. Then we could sit on someone's wall to eat them and throw the paper bags in the gutter when we've finished.'

Marsh smiled and said, 'If you do, I shall have to arrest you both for contravening the litter law. I should take your wife to the Dining Room if I were you, sir.'

'I knew you were going to be trouble when you took that last slice of cake, Marsh. All right, my love, you win. Give the Dining Room a ring and see if they've got a nice table for two.'

Jane gave a smile to Marsh. 'Thank you, Sergeant. I might be able to find another piece of cake if you can manage it.'

'Just for that, Marsh, you can ring the station and see if they know who is taking over from Roberts,' said Bill. 'I don't want to be stared at by a stranger while I'm eating.'

★　★　★

When Father O'Connor telephoned, Bill explained about Dave Norris's suggestion that he should be wired and was surprised that there was no objection to the idea.

'You realize that if you do this, nobody must know. And I mean nobody, especially the boys. You might be in danger, you understand that?

'I do, Inspector. It's the devil's work that they are doing and as a priest it is my duty to rid the streets of these evil men. Tell your friend on the drug squad to arrange things and I shall meet him somewhere.'

'I'll try and get him now and he can ring you while you're at home.' Bill rang off and called Dave Norris on his mobile. 'Hello, Dave. I have just spoken to Father O'Connor and he has no objection to meeting you to discuss his being wired.'

'That's great, Bill. Now where shall I meet him?'

'Well, it mustn't be anywhere that you're known. The last thing we want is for him to be seen speaking to a copper. I don't want these people arranging an accident for him.'

'I had thought about that and wondered if he would feel happier with another man of the church.'

'Who have you got in mind?'

'Me. And before you say anything, let me tell you I look very convincing wearing a dog collar. I've done it before.'

Bill tried to suppress a laugh. 'I'm sure you have.'

'I can hear you busting a gut trying not to laugh,' said Dave. 'But let me tell you, disguise is an important part of my job.'

'Sorry, Dave, but I was trying to imagine

you dressed as a priest, that's all. But seriously, if you looked like a priest you could meet him quite openly at the club, or better still, a quiet restaurant. What would be more natural than two priests having a meal together?'

'I like it.'

'Good. I'll give you his home number and you can ring him now and make arrangements.'

Bill gave him Father O'Connor's phone number and wished him luck then looked at Marsh, who had just finished his call to Chelsea police station.

'Well?'

'Don Walker is taking over from Roberts. You know him — he's the stocky fellow with a Yorkshire accent,' said Marsh. 'Looks like a rugby player.'

'The big man. I know.' Bill got up, opened the door and called, 'Have you managed to book the table, Jane?'

'Yes. It's booked for eight o'clock,' she replied.

'Thanks, love.' He closed the door and sat down. 'I can't offer you a drink, Sergeant, because you're driving.'

'That's all right, sir.'

'I was going to say come and join us tonight, but I imagine you've got other plans.'

'Yes. Sally is cooking dinner tonight.'

31

'I'm glad you two are getting on. She's a nice girl, Marsh. Be good to her.'

'I will.' He smiled.

Bill got up and poured himself a whisky. 'No news on Bob Plummer when you rang the nick just now?'

'I did ask but so far they've not heard anything.'

Bill sat down again and sipped his drink. 'I wish they knew where the bloody man is. You would think it was impossible for a man like him to just walk out of prison, beat up a policeman and disappear.'

'He'll make a mistake. They always do sooner or later,' Marsh said with conviction.

'Well, I hope it's sooner. The last thing I want is to go out to dinner with my wife plus an armed copper,' said Bill.

★   ★   ★

When Father O'Connor heard Dave Norris's suggestion that he too would dress as a priest and that they met at a quiet restaurant, it tickled his sense of humour.

'I think it's a wonderful idea, Inspector, especially when the police department are paying the bill.' He chuckled and added, 'That will include the wine, of course. We must look as though we are old friends

32

enjoying ourselves.'

Dave smiled to himself and said, 'It will certainly include the wine, Father. Inspector Forward didn't think you would mind wearing a concealed recorder.'

'On the contrary, I shall enjoy the experience. And I shall also get satisfaction in the knowledge that I am helping to rid our streets of these people.'

'Thank you, Father. Is it convenient for us to meet soon? I can then show you the recorder and you will see how very easy it is to conceal. But whatever you do, don't let anyone know you are wearing one.'

'Don't worry. Inspector Forward explained the dangers to me. I was wondering which restaurant we should meet at. Have you tried that new Italian one just off the Kings Road? Apparently they do a very nice house wine.'

'Yes, I know the one. Are you free tonight?'

'I can be. The boys invite their friends round to play snooker and I like to be there to lock up. But I suppose I can get one of the boys to do so if I'm not there. Terry Kennedy is very reliable so I shall ask him to do it. The restaurant is open from six o'clock on Saturdays.'

'All right, Father. Let's make it tonight. I'll arrange for a table. Will seven o'clock be too early for you?'

'Seven is fine and I shall look forward to seeing you there.' Father O'Connor hung up and began to wonder what the inspector would look like when he arrived at the restaurant dressed as a priest, and the thought amused him.

★　★　★

Bob Plummer was released on bail after serving just half of his five-year sentence. He had not caused any trouble and had his sentence cut on the technicality of good behaviour. While in prison, Plummer heard that his wife had packed up and moved from London to the Brighton area, but none of his contacts knew if she was staying alone or with somebody else. Plummer was convinced she had a man somewhere and the thought of her in bed with another man made him angry. He was determined to find them once he was free and teach them both a lesson they would never forget. And this time he would make sure he didn't get caught.

He would find the two policemen who came to her rescue and whose evidence got him put inside. In his opinion they were interfering in a marital argument and should be taught that it didn't pay to come between a man and his wife, especially when the man was Bob Plummer. First he would find Constable Lockhart. And when he had finished with him he would look for Sergeant Forward. He would find him wherever he was and get retribution for the time he had been in prison. These were promises he made to himself when he was locked up.

And now he was free and had used his cunning to find Lockhart. He waited in a quiet alley for the policeman to make his way home. Using brute strength he hit Lockhart and enjoyed hearing him cry out in pain. After Lockhart was unconscious he ran off to find somewhere safe to stay. It had to be somewhere he could hide for a while and he knew the perfect place. A friend he had met in prison had a caravan he could use. It was on a site in Kent and a phone call was all it took to use it. His friend rang the manager of the site and instructed him to give Plummer the key when he arrived. Plummer would stay there until his moustache had grown and his hair was longer and dyed to cover the grey. Then he would wear a pair of spectacles and look completely different. He was convinced he could then go out without anyone ever recognizing him. And that's when he would make Sergeant Forward regret that he had ever made an enemy of Bob Plummer.

4

Jane Forward was getting ready in the bedroom when she heard a car starting up outside. She looked out of the window and saw Constable Roberts drive away and another car take the space. As she finished dressing, the phone rang and she heard her husband answer it. By the time she got down to the front room, he was speaking.

'Yes, that's the one. We shall be leaving here in a few minutes, so we'll see you there.' He hung up and spoke to Jane, who was looking curious. 'That was Walker. He's just replaced Roberts for the night shift.'

'Poor man,' said Jane. 'Has he got to sit out there all night?'

'I'm afraid so.'

'Can't he come and sit in here? At least he would be more comfortable than sitting in a car.'

'I know. And if it was just for tonight I would agree, love. But what if they don't pick up Plummer for a few more days? Walker would become our lodger.'

'I hadn't thought of that. But what if he needs to use the toilet?'

Bill smiled and said, 'I *had* thought of that.'

'So what would he do?'

'I shall give him a spare key and he can use the one in the cloakroom down here. Can we go now or have you got any more questions?'

'Well, if he does have to come in I shall probably wake up and think we've got burglars.'

Bill gave an upward look of despair. 'In that case dial 999 and ask for a policeman. Come on.'

He ushered Jane out of the house and into the car, for what he hoped would be a pleasant evening at the Dining Room restaurant.

★   ★   ★

Constable Walker had studied the photograph of Plummer and had his face fixed in his mind. He waited for Bill to arrive and park in one of the spaces provided at the side of the restaurant for customers only. Walker had parked near the entrance to the car park and displayed a disabled card on the windscreen. He got out of his car and followed Bill and his wife, having satisfied himself that there was no sign of Plummer. He walked into the Dining Room just as Bill was being shown to the table and waited to see where he and Jane would be sitting. He saw that if he could have the table laid for two near the bar he would have a good view of Bill, the door, and the entire restaurant. He turned to the girl standing by the desk and smiled as he said, 'I'm a doctor and may get a call to leave in a hurry. Although I am alone, is it possible for me to sit at this table?'

After a moment's hesitation, she returned his smile. 'Yes, of course, Doctor.' While she was making it a table for one, Walker caught the eye of Bill Forward, who mimed washing his hands. He walked to the gentleman's toilet and went in. Satisfied that there was nobody else in there, he waited. A few moments later Bill came in.

'It's OK to talk. There's no-one here,' Walker told him.

'Good. I want you to take this key and let yourself into my house if you need to. My downstairs cloakroom isn't as big as this one but it's more private.' Bill smiled and gave Walker the key.

'Thank you,' said Walker.

They heard somebody coming and Bill put his hands under the dryer, while Walker washed his and watched a young man go into a cubicle. Bill left and went back to join his wife.

* * *

Father O'Connor called at the club and asked Terry Kennedy to lock up if he wasn't back in time. He then made his way to the restaurant, looking forward to his meeting with Inspector Norris.

Dave Norris had not worn anything elaborate, just a grey suit and dog collar. But his appearance was convincing. He arrived at the restaurant and was able to sit at a corner table where he would be able to say what he had to quietly and without being overheard. He looked at the menu and was wondering what he would order when he noticed his dinner companion arrive. He waved to Father O'Connor and stood to greet him as a waiter escorted him to the table. Father O'Connor shook hands with him and both men sat as the waiter left them.

Father O'Connor smiled. 'You look remarkably well, Father.'

Dave felt he was being complimented on the way he was dressed and gave a nod of gratitude. 'Shall we have a drink before we order the food?'

Father O'Connor gave a saucy grin as he said, 'What a civilized suggestion. I understand the house red is rather nice.'

Dave attracted the waiter's attention and ordered it.

After they had ordered their food and could sit without interruption, Dave produced an innocent-looking biro pen and passed it to Father O'Connor. In a quiet voice he said, 'Clip this safely into the top pocket of your jacket, and the conversation with anyone in your vicinity can be recorded. All you need to do is press down the top, as you would to begin writing, and the recording will start.'

'Good heavens. You mean this pen is really a recorder!'

'Yes. It will run for approximately one hour, which should be long enough for anyone to say what they are up to and, without realizing it, condemn themselves. Do you think you can manage that?'

'Oh yes. I shall get pleasure from it.'

'But be careful. Don't let anyone know that you have this pen, especially the boys. If anyone asks to borrow it, say it is out of ink and needs a refill. Do you understand?'

'I do.'

Their conversation came to an abrupt end as their soup arrived. During the meal they discussed everything except the pen and Dave hoped the meeting would be worthwhile. As soon as they had finished eating, Dave paid the bill and when they got to their cars, Dave gave Father O'Connor his card.

'This is my mobile number. If you have a problem, don't hesitate to ring. And remember, that pen will pick up any conversation within a few feet so you don't need to get too close to anyone. Be careful, Father. And thanks for coming.'

'Thank you for the meal and don't worry, I'll be fine.'

They shook hands and went their separate ways.

On his way home, Father O'Connor was disappointed he hadn't had a practical demonstration of the recorder. He felt like a child with a new toy, wishing he could have played with it and heard what it sounded like. He now hoped he would soon be able to put the pen to good use.

★   ★   ★

Bill had enjoyed his meal and was relaxing with a coffee.

'That was lovely,' he said, as he gave his stomach a gratified pat.

'Thanks for bringing me here. I know it's expensive but it doesn't hurt to push the boat out once in a while,' said Jane, smiling.

'I don't begrudge a penny of it tonight, love. That was one of the best steaks I've had. I just hope Don Walker didn't have one. He'd never get away with that on his expenses.' Bill grinned. He finished his coffee and ordered another.

'I know you would like a brandy with it,' said Jane. 'I've only had two glasses of wine, so I'll drive home if you like.'

'That's very kind of you, love. But at the price this place charges, I'd rather have a brandy at home.'

Jane looked around at the other tables and said, 'I know they are expensive and not often full here on a Saturday, but they've got a lot of people in tonight.'

'Yes. But there is one person that didn't call in tonight.'

'Who's that?'

'The man Walker and I would like to get our hands on, Bob Plummer.'

'I've had such a nice evening I'd forgotten about him. Do you think they've caught him yet?'

'I'm sure I would have heard if they had. Don't worry about Plummer, love. Let's go home and I can sit in comfort with a nice brandy.'

'All right, we'll go home and I'll sit with you and have a nice vodka and tonic.' Jane smiled as she added, 'That will be cheaper at home as well.'

Seeing them getting ready to leave, Walker

paid his bill and went outside. He waited for them to get into their car then went to his and followed them home.

★   ★   ★

It was just before nine o'clock the following morning when Roberts arrived as Walker's replacement. Being Sunday, the road was quiet as Walker drove away and when Bill heard the cars he looked out and saw Roberts park. Bill wished he could have gone to the office. He felt like a fit man claiming sick leave and Superintendent Lamb's order that he should stay at home until Plummer had been caught was making him irritable. He had finished his breakfast and Jane was clearing the table when his mobile rang. He picked it up and heard Terry Kennedy's voice. He sounded anxious.

'Hello, Mr Forward, it's Terry.'

'Is something wrong, lad?'

'I don't know.'

'What do you mean?'

'Well, it's Father O'Connor. I went to open the club in case he wasn't there this morning and it was open but no sign of him. His office was open too. I called him but there wasn't any reply. And there's something else.'

'What's that?'

'I thought I saw that man driving away. The one I picked out of the photographs that Inspector Norris showed me.'

'Benny Sutherland?' asked Bill anxiously.

'Yes.'

Bill didn't hesitate. 'Stay there, Terry. I'll be right over.'

He quickly explained to Jane, then got into his car and drove off, giving Roberts a wave as he went. He was going to give Dave Norris a call but decided to wait until he had spoken to Father O'Connor. He called Marsh and explained what he was doing.

'Do you want me to come over?' asked Marsh.

'No point until I find out what's going on. I've got Roberts following me and we don't want to arrive like the cavalry at full charge. I'll let you know what's happening as soon as I know myself,' Bill said and rang off.

It didn't take long for him to arrive at the club. As he parked he heard a siren and saw an ambulance drive past him and turn into the side road. Bill got out of his car and as he heard the siren being switched off he had a gut feeling and hurried into the side road. When he saw Terry standing there, looking frightened, he knew what to expect. Lying on the pavement was Father O'Connor. He was unconscious and there was blood coming from his head. The paramedics got to work immediately to stop the bleeding. Bill put a fatherly arm around Terry.

'Don't worry, lad. Once they get him to the hospital he'll be as good as new. I take it you called the ambulance.'

'Yes. I phoned you and then went outside to see if Father O'Connor might have gone out for something. He will be all right, won't he, Mr Forward?'

'Of course he will. Go and put the kettle on and make some coffee. I'll be in as soon as I find out which hospital they are taking him to.'

As Terry walked away, Constable Roberts came up to Bill.

'What happened?' asked Roberts.

'I don't know. But a certain Benny Sutherland was seen here earlier and maybe he was involved. He's been trying to get some of the boys here interested in the goods that he peddles.'

'What sort of goods?'

'The ones you sniff or stick in your veins,' Bill said quietly to avoid being heard by the paramedics.

'Christ. And what sort of scum would do that to a priest?'

'Scum like Benny Sutherland,' said Bill. Then he turned to the paramedics. 'Which

45

hospital are you taking him to?'

'Chelsea and Westminster,' one replied.

Bill produced his warrant card. 'I'm DI Forward. Tell your people that I shall be along soon. Come on, Roberts, let's get a coffee.'

As they went to the club, Father O'Connor was lifted on to a stretcher and put in the ambulance. It left with the siren switched on again.

'It's a pity there are only old warehouses where the attack took place. Otherwise we might have had a witness to it,' Bill mused as he looked up the road.

Terry made coffee for them, and as Bill took his cup he said, 'How long ago was it that you thought you saw Benny Sutherland, Terry?'

'Not long before I phoned you. Do you think he did that to Father O'Connor?'

'I won't know what really happened until I can speak to the Father myself. I'll get over to the hospital soon but I'll give them time to tend to his head and get him comfortable before I try to talk to him. I can't put out an APB on Benny until I know for certain who actually struck the Father. By the way, Terry, this is Constable Roberts. So if you see him around you will know he's not one of Benny Sutherland's friends. But don't tell the other boys he's a policeman.'

'Pleased to meet you, Mr Roberts,' said Terry.

'Likewise, Terry,' said Roberts. 'Nice coffee, by the way.'

'Thank you.'

'It's very quiet here this morning, Terry,' said Bill.

'The boys will soon be arriving. There's a snooker match on at 10.30. Do I tell them what happened to Father O'Connor? Only they are sure to wonder why he isn't here.'

'Just tell them he had a meeting to go to and that he left you in charge. I will phone you here once I know what the situation is at the hospital and tell you what to say. Until then, just carry on as normal,' Bill told him.

'All right,' said Terry.

Bill and Roberts finished their drinks and went to their cars. As they drove away Bill called Marsh and told him what had happened.

'I thought Superintendent Lamb ordered you to stay home. But I imagine it slipped your mind, sir,' Marsh said.

'Yes, it did. Oh dear, aren't I naughty? I'll tell him when I get home and he might forgive me. Meanwhile I shall make sure Father O'Connor is all right and hope he can tell me who attacked him. If he does I'll get an APB put out on them. I'll call you later.'

As Bill drove on he could see Roberts in the car behind him. But he hadn't noticed that another car was following them at a safe distance, and that the driver of that car was Benny Sutherland.

★ ★ ★

Superintendent Gilbert of the Kent Constabulary was at his desk when Inspector Harris came to his office.

'What is it, Harris?'

'Constable Morley was following some boys he suspected of stealing a dog in Oaklea Woods. When they spotted him they made a run for it.'

'Does he know who they were?'

'Oh yes,' said Harris. 'He caught up with them at the caravan site and got the names of two of the boys and found out where the dog was.'

The superintendent wondered why Harris was bothering to report what appeared to be an unimportant case to him. 'All's well that ends well then.'

'Yes, sir, but the thing is, while Morley was there he saw the caravan that belonged to Roy Galloway, who got out of prison recently. Morley saw the site manager come out of the caravan with a black bin liner full of rubbish that had been left there. He told Morley that a friend of Galloway had been staying there and that the man had left this morning without saying anything. He just dropped the key in the letterbox and went. He described the man as a big chap with the tattoo of a dolphin on his left arm. Morley looked through the rubbish bag and found an empty bottle of hair dye. Morley thought the description was similar to the APB for a Bob Plummer, put out by the Met. I made a phone call and discovered that Plummer had been with Galloway in the same prison. I wanted to let you know before taking it upon myself to call our colleagues up in Chelsea. In case you would rather do that yourself, sir.'

Superintendent Gilbert smiled. 'That's very diplomatic of you, Harris. But I think you have earned the right to make that call. Send Morley to me. I would like to congratulate him personally for his part in this.'

'I will. And thank you, sir.'

'And I think you should get the site manager to let one of our chaps have a look around the contents of that caravan. In case there might be something else there that would be useful to us and our colleagues in the Met.'

'I'll get on to it right away, sir.'

★ ★ ★

Bob Plummer was pleased with the reflection that he saw of himself in the mirror. The new moustache and dyed hair had changed his appearance considerably. As he was in Kent, he wished he had the address where his wife was staying and who it was she was with. If, as he suspected, it was another man, he would like to pay her a surprise visit. But he had no idea where in the Brighton area she might be and decided to leave her until later. With his new appearance, he would soon be ready to find the policeman he knew as Sergeant Forward and pay *him* a visit. He was going to enjoy showing him that it didn't pay to put Bob Plummer behind bars. Now he would get on the train and enjoy his journey, and would not be recognized by anyone looking for him. Of that he was convinced.

★ ★ ★

Bill Forward sat beside Father O'Connor's bed and Roberts waited outside his room. The Father's head had been bandaged with a dressing over the wound made by the blow he had received. He opened his eyes and realized he had a visitor.

His voice was tired and weak. 'Hello, Inspector. I'm sorry. I must have dozed off.'

'I'm not going to keep you, Father. But do you know who hit you?'

'No. Whoever it was came at me from behind, so I have no idea who it was.' Putting his hand up to his head, he felt the bandage. 'Good Lord! What must I look like?'

Bill smiled and said, 'At the moment, the model for a new style of crash helmet.'

'No wonder the National Health are losing money. Surely a plaster would have sufficed?' said the Father.

'You needed eight stitches,' said Bill. 'It was a nasty bang you received. It's a pity you don't know who did it. Striking a priest is unforgivable.'

'Whoever it was will be punished for their sins when they come face to face with God.'

'I would like to punish them before they get that far,' said Bill as he got to his feet.

'Are you leaving already?'

'You need rest.'

'It was nice of you to come, Inspector. It's nice to have a visitor.'

'Terry will want to come and see you. He was the lad that found you and called the ambulance.'

'I would like to see him. I hope he is managing at the club. I didn't want so much responsibility being thrust on him.'

'You mustn't worry about Terry. He's a capable lad and I'm sure he won't let you down. Now close your eyes and rest.'

'I will. I will.' His voice was tired and he smiled as he gave a weak wave. Bill closed the door quietly and left. He went to his car and as he and Roberts started their engines, Bill caught a brief glimpse in his mirror of the driver of another car in the row behind. He was certain he had seen the man before and just as he was about to turn into the way out lane he looked in his mirror again. He saw the man leaving his car and go to the hospital entrance. Bill quickly turned his car and headed slowly to a parking bay. Roberts did the same, wondering what the inspector was doing. As they got out of their vehicles, Bill went up to Roberts.

'I've just remembered who the man parked behind us was. It's Benny Sutherland, the drug dealer that was seen driving away from the area where the priest was attacked.'

'Are you sure?' said Roberts.

'Yes. We've got his mugshot back in the office, but what I want to know is, what is he doing here? I'm going back to Father O'Connor's room in case Benny pays him a visit. You wait here, and if he makes a run for it, grab him.'

Roberts gave an affirmative nod. 'If he does I'll be ready for him.'

Bill hurried back into the hospital and as he did so he saw Sutherland making enquiries at the desk. Keeping out of sight, Bill was surprised when Sutherland smiled at the receptionist and walked back to the car park. Bill went to the receptionist and showed his warrant card. 'What did that man want?'

'He asked how the priest was and whether he could visit him. I told him he was doing well but not up to having any visitors at the moment — perhaps this afternoon,' she said.

'That man must not be allowed to visit Father O'Connor. I shall arrange for a police officer to keep guard outside his room. Until he gets here there must be no other visitors.'

'I understand,' she said.

Bill went to the main entrance and saw Sutherland drive away. Roberts gave an enquiring look as Bill walked over to him. 'I'm going to arrange for a PC to keep guard on Father O'Connor's room before I go home.' He went to his car and got through to the duty sergeant and made arrangements for a PC to get over to the hospital as soon as possible. Bill could see that he had a voicemail and when he looked to see who had called, wondered why Superintendent Lamb wanted to speak to him. Bill got straight through, hoping it was to tell him Bob Plummer had been found and arrested.

'DI Forward here, sir. You wanted me.'

'Yes, Forward, where the devil are you?'

'I'm just leaving the Chelsea and Westminster hospital, sir. Father O'Connor is in there. Someone beat him over the head this morning and although he doesn't know who it was, it could be Benny Sutherland. He's been to make enquiries about him at the hospital and I've arranged for a PC to guard the Father's room. And don't worry about me, sir. Roberts was with me all the time.'

'But I do worry about you, Forward. I've had some news about Plummer.'

'Do you know where he is?' Bill asked hopefully.

'No. But we know where he's been. He's been staying at a caravan site in Kent. Apparently he has been using hair dye, so we think he's no longer grey but brown. And he's grown a moustache which we must assume is also brown.'

'Then we must get our art people to doctor one of our photographs of Plummer to give us an idea of what he looks like now.'

'They are doing that as we speak. I shall get a copy sent out with our chaps and one each for you, Roberts and Marsh. I'm also getting it distributed in the Met and our people in the Brighton area. That's where his ex-wife is staying with her new boyfriend apparently. Plummer might be stupid enough to go looking for her there. But my main concern is to keep you from getting beaten up.'

'I appreciate that, sir. But I would like to get back to work in the morning. I'll have Roberts and Marsh to keep our friend Plummer from getting too close. And let's face it, I've got to get back otherwise I might just as well take an early retirement and I am not ready for that just yet.'

'I know. And I don't want to lose you, so come back in the morning but be bloody careful.'

'I will, thank you, sir.'

'I shall send Marsh to your home with the new image of what we think Plummer might look like. Keep your eyes open and if you see him, don't be a hero. Put out a call for assistance.'

'Don't worry, I will,' Bill said as he rang off. On his way home he became worried about Jane being alone while he was back at work. He was thinking about the day he was called to Plummer's wife after he had beaten her so badly around the face. He knew that Plummer could be a threat to Jane if he knew she was alone in the house and that he would have no hesitation about hitting a woman. The thought began to nag at him and he made up his mind that in the morning he would discuss with Lamb the possibility of some protection for his wife.

5

The photograph of Bob Plummer had surprised DI Forward and he sat looking at it in disbelief.

'I know,' his sergeant agreed. 'Without seeing that photo of him, neither would I. It's amazing what a bit of hair dye and a moustache can do to change an appearance. He even looks younger.'

'That's why so many women colour their hair, Marsh, so that they can win the heart of a young man such as you.' Then he added, 'I'll show this to Jane. Then if she sees this face at the front door she'll know not to open it. With this photograph in circulation he can't remain free for long, surely?'

'Unless he decides to grow a beard, then we won't know *who* we're looking for,' said Marsh.

'That's right, cheer me up, Sergeant.'

'I'm sorry but it's true. Plummer is a clever bugger to have stayed free in a caravan park of all places. Then he disappears again like the invisible man. Didn't the Kent lads say he was staying in the caravan belonging to a chap he was in prison with?'

'Yes, a Roy Galloway. He was released

about the same time as Plummer. Our Kent colleagues have kept a close eye on Galloway but he and Plummer have not made any contact with each other as far as they know. I tell you, this whole business is bloody frustrating. I'll get Jane to make us a coffee. Then I can show her this photograph of the man who is becoming my nemesis.'

'What *is* a nemesis?'

'It's a Greek word for retribution, or vengeance, Sergeant. But with your education I would have thought you'd know that. You'll have to study your Greek if you want to make it to inspector one day,' Bill said with a straight face.

Marsh knew Bill was being sarcastic and retorted, 'So old Baa-Baa must be fluent in the language. Otherwise he would never have made it to superintendent, would he, sir?'

Bill smiled and said, 'Touché. And that's French. Now, we deserve a coffee, I think.' He called to Jane and asked her to make some coffee. Then he showed her the new photograph of Bob Plummer. Once she had left the room he told Marsh about his intention to ask the super for some protection for Jane.

'It's a good idea. You never know what that bastard might do while he's on the loose,' Marsh told him. 'I can't believe he's still free and out there somewhere, but where?'

Bill looked anxious as he said, 'Yes, where?'

★ ★ ★

The woman on the train sat opposite Plummer and when he asked to borrow her newspaper she passed it to him with a smile. She was in her early thirties and quite attractive. While he was reading, he glanced up at her occasionally and could see her looking at him with a smile that told him she was interested in knowing him better. After a while, he passed the newspaper back to her.

'Are you sure you have finished looking?' she asked.

'At the paper, yes,' he replied.

'Is there something else you would rather look at?' she asked in an unmistakably suggestive but quiet tone.

He leaned towards her and said in an equally quiet and suggestive voice, 'If we were alone, we could probably find things that we would both enjoy looking at. But sadly we are not alone. And I imagine your day is taken care of.'

'Is yours?'

'No. I have nothing to do that can't wait. And especially if we could find time to be alone together.'

She took a piece of paper from her handbag and wrote on it. 'This is where I shall be staying tonight. If you're free around 7.30, give me a ring. My name's Pat, by the way.'

He took the piece of paper from her and read what she had written. It said: *Miss Harrison, Morgan Hotel, Clapham.* Beside the hotel she had scribbled the telephone number. He checked it with her to make sure that he had read it correctly and put the paper in his pocket.

'Thank you, Pat. I'm Bob.' He took her hand and as he gently shook it, stroked her palm with his index finger, to which she responded by doing the same to him. This told him he was getting an offer of sex and he was determined to take it. As the train pulled into Clapham Junction he got up and lifted her case from the rack above her head. He carried it to the door and as she took it she pursed her lips, mimed a kiss and said, 'Call me.'

'I will. And we can get together tonight.'

He watched her walk down the platform and couldn't believe that this attractive stranger made him feel so very certain he would be having exciting sex before the evening was over. His original plan to find a Sergeant Forward could wait until he knew

60

where his relationship with Pat might lead. On arrival at Charing Cross station, he made his way to the friend he had arranged to spend his time in London with — a private investigator with a shady past, Joe Levin.

When Plummer arrived at the apartment in Soho, he remembered the first time he'd seen it and how proud he had been to know someone that lived in the centre of London. Levin's father had bought it freehold many years earlier and Joe knew it was an impressive address for his work. It was also an address that allowed him to charge big fees to clients that came to him for his professional services. Joe first met Plummer when he used him as a bodyguard when carrying valuables. It wasn't long before Plummer was one of Joe's regular minders but his recent spell in prison meant that Plummer's run of earning himself a lot of money had come to a sudden halt. All he could do now was hope Joe Levin hadn't replaced him on a permanent basis. Keeping his fingers crossed, he rang the doorbell.

Joe Levin checked his visitor's identity on his internal CCTV screen and opened the door. He shook Plummer by the hand and gave a welcoming smile as he quickly got him into the hallway and closed the door.

'Come in, Bob. I don't want anyone to see

you coming here. Might be a problem, you understand.'

'I don't think anyone will recognize me.'

'Well, I wouldn't have if you hadn't told me about the dyed hair and the moustache when you phoned me. Can't be too careful though,' said Joe, trying to sound relaxed. 'You do know there's an all-ports bulletin out on you, I suppose?'

'Bound to be, but not the new Bob Plummer.' He grinned as he stroked his hair and tickled his moustache playfully.

'Apparently there is a photograph of you with your hair that colour *and* the moustache.'

Plummer looked shocked as he said, 'You've got to be joking!'

'No, Bob, I'm not. A friend of mine at the police station told me. He knew I was planning to let you stay here while you were in London, and warned me. He keeps me up to date with what's going on, especially if he thinks it will help me with a case I'm working on. So you see your staying here is out of the question now. If it was known you were here I would lose my licence.'

'But how the hell did they know about my dyed hair? I only went out after it was done and . . . ' He suddenly thought of something and angrily thumped his fist on the arm of the chair. 'Bugger it! I meant to throw the dye containers away but I was in such a hurry to leave the caravan I forgot! That site manager must have found them and told the police.'

'Or the police had a tip-off and *they* found them. But it doesn't change the fact that I can't have you staying here. You can understand that.'

Plummer reluctantly agreed with a grunt. 'Yeah.'

'What were you coming to London for, anyway?'

'I wanted to look up a copper named Forward and say thank you for getting me put inside,' he said with bitter sarcasm. 'I was hoping you would find out where he was for me.'

'You mean you intended to sort him out, physically?'

'The bastard cost me my marriage and my freedom so I owe him one,' he said as he banged his right fist hard into his left hand. 'I want to watch him suffer like I did.'

'For Christ's sake, have you taken leave of your senses? Do that and you'll spend the rest of your life behind bars! The law doesn't take kindly to police officers being beaten up.' Joe wanted Plummer out of his apartment before he caused trouble. 'Have you got somewhere else you can go tonight?'

Plummer remembered Pat's invitation and smiled. 'As a matter of fact, I have. An attractive young lady I met on the train has invited me to have dinner with her. So I shall get a taxi to the station and a train to Clapham.'

'How are you off for money, Bob?'

'I haven't got much in my account but I've got a credit card. That should keep me going until I can get to a bank in the morning.'

Joe took a wad of notes from his pocket and counted out a £100, which he pushed into Plummer's hand.

'Take that and let me have a contact number in case a job comes up that I can put your way.'

Plummer took the money and became more cheerful. 'I really am sorry I won't be staying here tonight. But with a bit of luck I might have more pleasure with my new female companion. Thanks for the money, Joe.' Plummer went to the front door and waited for Joe to open it.

Joe saw Plummer out of the apartment, careful that no-one saw him leave. Being a Sunday, there weren't many people about and although he was relieved to say goodbye to his visitor, he hoped he would not get picked up by the police before he had enjoyed an evening with his new ladyfriend.

Pat Harrison was in her room going through a list of calls she had to make tomorrow when the telephone rang.

'Pat Harrison.'

'This is Bob. I'm at Victoria station and thought I would ring and see if our getting together tonight is still on.'

'That would be nice,' she said in a quiet voice. 'What have you got in mind?'

'I thought we could have a meal somewhere. And then see how we feel. How does that grab you?'

'That all depends where you grab me,' she said in a very provocative way, then added, 'As long as you're not *too* rough.'

He became sexually excited and replied, 'Oh, I would only do what you wanted, how you wanted.' His breathing was becoming more rapid as he waited for her to speak.

'Why don't you come here? They have a nice restaurant. Or have you somewhere else in mind?'

'No. Your hotel sounds fine. Perhaps they could find a room for me. The place where I was going to stay is closed.'

'Well, you come here then. I'm sure finding you a place to sleep won't be a problem. Do you want me to book a table?'

'That would be nice. Seven thirty OK?'

'Yes. I'll book it now. And you can use my bathroom to wash when you get here and see how you feel about getting a room later.'

'So what time shall I come over?'

'I shall be finished with my paperwork by five, so any time from then and we can have a drink and you can tell me what you do for a living.'

'And you must tell me what you do, Pat. I shall see you about five o'clock then.'

'I look forward to it.' She hung up, wondering what she would learn about the stranger she had found so sexually intriguing.

★ ★ ★

Bill Forward's mobile rang and he was surprised to hear what the duty sergeant had to tell him.

'Among the rubbish they found in the caravan, the lads in Kent found a piece of paper with a name and address on it. Although it was all screwed up and the writing was not that clear, they said it was an address in Soho and thought it might be important.'

'What's the name and address?'

'As far as they can make out it's Joe Levin, Abbey Court, Soho. And if my memory serves me correctly, Joe Levin is a private eye with a reputation for bending the law when it suits him. He might be worth a visit, sir.'

'I will certainly call on Mr Levin. Thank you, Sergeant.'

'Good luck, sir.'

Bill rang off and looked for Joe Levin's name in the London telephone directory. Within seconds he found it and called Marsh's number.

'I have just received the name and address of a private eye that might know where Bob Plummer is, so I'm going to give him a call. If he's there I shall pay him a visit. I'll call you and let you know if I'm lucky and we can meet there.'

'Where is it?'

'Abbey Court. It's an apartment block in Soho. Keep your fingers crossed, Sergeant. This could be the break we've been waiting for.'

Marsh wrote it down and hoped the search for Plummer would soon be at an end.

Bill dialled Levin's number and was glad to find him in.

'Is that Joe Levin?'

'Levin, speaking.'

'This is DI Forward, Chelsea. Will it be convenient to come over and see you, sir? I am hoping you will be able to help us with some inquiries.'

'Yes, of course.' Despite being worried,

Levin was able to sound unconcerned. 'I shall be only too pleased to help if I can. My apartment is number eighteen. I'm above the book shop.'

'Thank you, sir.'

'Can you tell me what your inquiry is regarding?'

'I would rather not do that over the telephone, sir. You know what they say, phones have ears. I won't be long.'

When Bill rang off, Joe had a feeling his inquiry was to do with Bob Plummer and didn't want to get on the wrong side of the law. He decided to protect himself by telling the truth if the inspector asked if Plummer had contacted him. At least he couldn't tell the police where Bob was because he genuinely had no idea.

Bill contacted Marsh and arranged to meet him in Soho. Then he called Roberts and told him where he was going but asked him to stay and keep an eye on Jane.

'My orders are to stay with you, sir,' said Roberts.

'I shall have Marsh with me.'

'Why not get him to stay with your wife while I am with you, sir? Then if Plummer should try and get at you I'll be where I am supposed to be. Besides, I'm armed and Marsh isn't.'

Bill knew he couldn't win the argument and gave in. 'I'll contact Marsh and tell him the change of plan. Let's go.'

★ ★ ★

When his doorbell rang, Levin managed to give his visitors a welcoming smile. Bill showed his warrant card, returned a friendly smile and introduced Roberts. Levin took them to the living room and they sat in the comfortable armchairs. Bill looked round the room and complimented Levin on his expensive and comfortable furnishings.

'This is where I bring my clients to convince them that I am worth my fee.' He grinned. 'Now, what can I do for you, Inspector?'

'I believe you know a Bob Plummer?'

'Yes. I used to call on his services when I was carrying anything of value from one place to another. He is a well-built man and my clients liked to know that their things were unlikely to be stolen while they were in my hands. Bob was not someone a thief would challenge.'

'So he was your minder,' Bill said.

'Yes and a good one. But then I heard he was given a prison sentence and I didn't hear from him again, until today. He telephoned to ask if he could stay here for a while. He said he had some business to attend to here in London. I told him it was out of the question.'

'So what was his reaction to that?'

'He was silent for a while and then said he did have another place he could stay that might be more pleasant. It was with a young woman who was staying in Clapham.'

'Did he say who this woman was?'

'No. He didn't mention her name. Just that she had said he could stay with her. I gather it was a sexual liaison.'

'Did he mention that he only got out of prison a few days ago and that he assaulted a police officer, causing serious physical injury?' Bill watched his reaction but was not sure if it was genuine.

'Bloody hell,' he said with surprise.

'So we've got an APB out for Plummer.'

Levin quickly said, 'I remember now. He boasted that he could go anywhere without being recognized. He said he looked years younger now. And that's why this woman he met on the train fancies him.'

'So he met her on a train. From where? Did he say?'

'No. I wasn't that interested. But if I had known there was an APB out on him I would have asked.'

'I'm sure you would, Mr Levin. If he

70

should contact you again, find out the woman's name and where she is, could you?' Bill asked as he got to his feet.

'Of course I will,' Levin said with a warm smile.

Bill gave him a card. 'This is my number at Chelsea nick. In case you should think of anything that might help us.'

Bill and Roberts were shown out and Levin closed the door with relief. He had now seen the policeman that Bob Plummer wanted to beat up. And although Roberts had sat quietly without saying anything, Joe Levin had noticed his jacket and had seen enough armed protection officers to know that he was one. Joe wished he knew a contact number for Bob, so that he could warn him about the armed policeman with Inspector Forward. But as it was, he decided to leave it and not get involved.

*   *   *

Bill was on his way home in the car when the call came to tell him that Father O'Connor was feeling better and would like to see him. Bill called Roberts and told him he was on his way to the hospital. When they arrived, the constable on guard outside the room confirmed that no visitors had called.

71

Bill went into the room and was pleased to see the patient sitting more upright and smiling.

'Thank you for coming, Inspector.'

'You look better sitting up with some pillows behind you. Almost angelic,' Bill said with a grin. 'Now what is it you want to see me about?'

'I suddenly remembered something about the person that hit me. As I went down I vaguely remember the shoes.'

'What about them?'

'Well, they were the kind that a woman would wear, but not a man — they were too fancy for a man.'

'How do you mean, fancy?'

'I remember they had brassy bits all over them.'

Bill smiled. 'So all we've got to do is hunt for a man or a woman with brassy bits on their shoes and we've solved the mystery of who hit you. Do you remember the colour of the shoes, by any chance?'

Father O'Connor tried hard to remember. 'Grey . . . I think. But I could be wrong. I might have just thought they were. I suppose they could have been a pale black.' He was now getting distressed at not remembering clearly.

'It could be the drugs they've given you for

your head wound,' Bill said kindly. 'You rest now and I'll come and see you tomorrow. And if anything else comes to mind, make a note of it and let me know when I come again.'

Bill left the room, hoping the bang on the head had not left the Father permanently confused.

★　★　★

When Bill got home he saw Marsh at the window and gave a wave of acknowledgement. As he opened his front door, Roberts parked outside. Jane came and greeted Bill.

'Sergeant Marsh asked if he could wait here for you. He's in the front room. I'll bring some coffee in,' she said.

'Thank you, love.'

Bill walked into the room and Marsh asked, 'What did he want?'

Bill sat in his armchair. 'To tell me that he thinks the person who hit him had some funny shoes on. He also thinks they were grey and had brass bits on them and might or might not belong to a woman but he can't be sure.'

'What does that mean?'

'It means that he is very confused. I want to speak to Terry at the club and see if he can remember anyone with shoes like that.' He suddenly remembered something. 'Hang on! Father O'Connor isn't the only one that's become confused. But I haven't had a bang on the head so I don't have an excuse.'

'What are you talking about?'

'Shoes, Sergeant. Unless I'm very much mistaken, Benny Sutherland's friend, Mike Long, wears fancy shoes.'

'You mean Mike Long, the drug dealer?'

'The very same, and he's not averse to violence if my memory serves me right. He runs a legitimate agency for house minders but it's in his wife's name, so officially he is not involved. But we know he's up to his eyes in anything he thinks he can get away with. And that includes drugs. I think somebody should have a chat with him and find out where he was yesterday when the Father was beaten. And what shoes he was wearing. I'm particularly interested in the shoes. If they match Father O'Connor's description of his assailant, we can bring him in.'

'Well, you can't go and see him — he'll recognize you.'

'I know. But a woman officer in plain clothes might be able to get the information we want.'

'Who have you got in mind?'

'Barbara French. She's an experienced

copper and knows the drill. I'll have a word with her in the morning.'

Jane brought a tray of coffee and after Marsh had his, he went home, hoping Plummer would get picked up so that life with his inspector would get back to normal again.

★   ★   ★

It was just after 5 p.m. when Bob Plummer arrived at the Morgan Hotel, Clapham. He asked the receptionist to give Pat Harrison a ring and tell her he was there. The girl put the phone down and smiled as she said, 'Miss Harrison is expecting you, sir. She's in room seven on the first floor.'

Bob thanked her and made his way to the lift. When he got out he saw room seven and felt excited as he knocked on the door. Pat opened it and gave him a welcoming smile.

'You're a good timekeeper, Bob. I always think it shows that a person is reliable when they are on time. Come in.'

Bob went in and wasn't sure whether to kiss her or not. Pat closed the door and offered her cheek to him. He kissed her but she tried not to let him go any further by pushing him gently towards a small armchair. The room was a nice size with a double bed, wardrobe, two armchairs at a coffee table and a small refrigerator.

'Let's have a drink and talk for a while, Bob. We mustn't spoil the evening by rushing things. Don't you agree?'

'Yes, of course,' he said, trying to sound convincing.

'Sit down and I'll get us a drink. I've got whisky or gin and tonic. And there's ice in the fridge. But if you prefer a beer I can ring down for one. So what will it be?'

'Gin and tonic sounds nice before we eat. I might try a whisky after dinner, unless you kick me out, of course,' he said jokingly.

Pat poured two gin and tonics and smiled. Then she took some ice and two slices of lemon from the fridge and put them in the glasses. 'It doesn't taste right without ice and lemon, does it?' she said as she passed him the drink.

'I agree. I must say I'm impressed by the way you made the drinks. You're prepared for everything, aren't you?'

'I like to think so, Bob. Cheers.'

'Cheers.' He took a sip and gave a look of admiration. 'It's perfect. So tell me about yourself, Pat. What do you do for a living?'

She sat in the second small armchair and said, 'I try to find people for a firm of solicitors.'

'How do you mean, find people?'

'People that have been left money or articles by relatives or friends in a will but aren't aware of it.'

'It sounds interesting. I suppose you have to travel a lot.'

'Yes. Sometimes I go abroad but it's mostly in Britain.'

'It must be nice to tell people there's money coming their way because a maiden aunt or someone took a shine to them.'

'Yes, it is. What about you? What do you do to keep the wolf from the door?'

He had his answer ready. 'My partner and I run a detective agency in Soho,' he said convincingly.

'But you don't actually live in London, do you?' said Pat. 'I remember you saying the place where you normally stay was closed.'

'Yes. I used to stay at a small private hotel but they sold out to a Chinese restaurant. So now I'm hoping to find a small place. I like to keep away from the big hotels in case I get recognized by someone I'm keeping tabs on. We can't be too careful in our business.' He knew he sounded convincing and was ready for more questions.

'Is your work very dangerous, Bob?'

'Sometimes, but I know how to take care of myself,' he said with a confident smile. 'You have to in my game.'

'Yes, I imagine you do. The only private detectives I've ever seen are in American movies. I never thought I would meet a real one, though.'

'Well, you have now.' He raised his glass to her and said, 'Here's to you, Pat.'

She raised her glass to him and smiled. 'Here's to us.'

Pat could feel him staring at her as he downed his drink and liked the sexual feeling it gave her. She finished her gin and tonic and reached over to take his glass from him. 'Let me replenish our drinks.' She was determined not to allow her natural desire get the better of her.

He watched her bending over to get fresh ice from the fridge and said, 'You've got great legs, Pat. When I saw you on the train they were the first thing I noticed about you.'

'Yes, I remember you staring at them.' She smiled.

'Well, I like looking at lovely things,' he said quietly. 'And you are rather lovely. Have you ever been married?'

She gave him his glass and sat with hers, sipping it before replying. 'I came close once but no, I never married. How about you, Bob?'

'Yes, I married, but when I had to go away

for a while she buggered off. I think she's got a man somewhere but I've no idea where she is. Anyway, she claimed I knocked her about and went for a divorce. Of course, I never laid a finger on her but she had some bruises at the time so they believed her, and she won.'

'So where did she get the bruises from?'

He shrugged. 'Who knows? But not from me, Pat. I would never hit a woman.'

'Not even if you were in bed and she wanted you to slap her for a while?' she asked provocatively. 'I mean gently, of course, to give her extra sexual pleasure,' she added with sensual smile.

'You know how to make a man horny, don't you?'

'If you're feeling like that, perhaps we should go down to the bar and sit next to each other in one of their alcoves. You could tell me more about your exciting work.'

'I was thinking more of getting you into bed,' he said.

'We mustn't rush these things, Bob. We have the whole night ahead of us. Come on.'

He watched her get up. Then he reluctantly got up and followed her as she held the door open. They walked from the room and she took his arm and guided him down the stairs rather than take the lift. He knew that she was teasing him but decided to wait until they were back in her bedroom before he let his feelings run wild. He was sure that Pat as a lover would be well worth waiting for.

6

DI Forward had got to his office early and was pleased to be back at work again. When Marsh arrived, he was glad to see his boss looking happy after his weekend spent mainly at home.

'Good morning, sir. Nice to see you back in the office again.'

'Thank you, Marsh. It's nice of the super to *allow* me to come back again. And if I'm a good boy he might even let me stay.'

Marsh was used to his sarcasm and smiled. 'So what do you want to do first? Apart from having a coffee, I mean?'

'That sounds like a sensible idea. A nice coffee would go down a treat right now.'

'I said apart from the coffee, sir.'

'I shall go and see Superintendent Lamb when he gets in and try and get someone over to my place to keep an eye on Jane. Until Plummer is locked up again I want to feel that she's safe. And I left a message for WPC French to see me when she arrives. I want her to go and check Mike Long out, as we discussed yesterday.'

'Oh yes, the man with the fancy shoes who

you believe thumped Father O'Connor on the head.'

'Yes. Any chance of you getting me a coffee now?'

Marsh picked up the internal phone and called the canteen. 'Could we have two coffees in Inspector Forward's office, please?'

As Marsh hung up, Bill looked surprised. 'Don't tell me you're getting addicted too.'

'I'm afraid you are becoming a bad influence on me, sir. I used to drink mostly tea until I met you.'

'It could be worse, Sergeant. It could be cocoa.'

Marsh cringed. 'Oh, don't. It reminds me of my childhood. I had to drink it when I went to bed in the winter.'

Bill laughed. 'Funny the things you hate when you're young. I hated tapioca pudding.' Before he could say any more, his phone buzzed. It was Sergeant Cooper at the front desk.

'You asked me to let you know when the super came in. He's just arrived, sir.'

'Thank you, Sergeant.' He put the phone down and turned to Marsh. 'Keep the coffee hot for me. I'm off to see the super before he gets tied up with somebody else.'

Bill hurried out of the office and down the corridor, where he knocked on Superintendent Lamb's door and entered.

'Have you got a minute, sir?'

'Come on in, Forward. Sit down. Have you got some news for me?'

'I've come to see you about the possibility of protection for my wife, sir.'

Lamb looked surprised. 'Oh?'

'Yes, sir. All weekend I've had an armed protection officer watching over me and I'm very grateful to you. But now I'm back at my office, Jane is left on her own until I get home again. If Plummer finds out where I live he might threaten Jane and I don't want her to get hurt because he has this obsession to get revenge on me. So until he gets put away again, I'd feel happier if someone could keep an eye on her safety, sir.'

Lamb nodded. 'Yes, I see your point. I hadn't thought about your wife. Of course she mustn't be in any danger. I'll get a policewoman from firearms over to your place until you get home. She'll take care of her, don't worry.'

Bill was relieved. 'Thank you, sir, I'll call her and let her know what you're arranging.'

Bill returned to his office, where Marsh pointed to a mug of coffee on his desk.

'It only just arrived so it will still be hot. How did you get on with Baa-Baa?'

'He's getting a woman from firearms over to my place. I'm just going to let Jane know.'

Bill picked up his phone and rang Jane.

'Hello, love. You will be getting a policewoman coming over to stay with you until I get home. Superintendent Lamb doesn't want you being on your own while Plummer is still on the loose and neither do I. So don't open the door to anyone until she gets there, OK? I'll try not to be late. I've got to go — there's someone at my door now. Bye, love.'

Marsh opened the office door and WPC Barbara French came in. 'I was told that Inspector Forward wanted to see me.'

'Yes, I do,' said Bill. 'I've a job I want you to do for me.' Bill gave her the reason for the enquiry he wanted made and told her all he knew about Mike Long, emphasizing the importance of the shoes. 'But you must be careful how you approach this Mike Long. If it *was* him that hit the priest, he wouldn't hesitate to hit a woman, so be on your guard.'

'He sounds a charming fellow.' She was thoughtful for a moment, then said, 'If he's as conceited about his clothes as it sounds, then he no doubt claims everything he wears for business expenses. So I could say I'm from the Inland Revenue checking what it is that he claims for. Men like him are more afraid of the tax inspector than the police, so I don't think he would be stupid enough to hit me. Do you, sir?'

'I don't care what you call yourself just as

84

long as you are careful,' said Bill. 'Sergeant Cooper at the front desk will give you the only address we've got for Mike Long.'

'I'll get on it right away, sir.' She smiled at Marsh as he held the door open for her. 'Thank you, Sergeant.'

When she had gone, Marsh closed the door and said, 'I can see why you chose her, sir. She didn't seem bothered when you told her that Long might not hesitate to hit her.'

'I hope for his sake he doesn't try. She's a black belt.'

'You mean in karate?'

'Yes.'

'So the poor bugger wouldn't know what hit him. That's why you told her he might attempt to hit her, so now she'll be ready for him.' Marsh smiled.

'Yes, and I'd like to have her around when Bob Plummer shows up. I don't think he would ever hit a woman again. If only we knew where the hell he was,' said Bill.

★ ★ ★

The Morgan Hotel in Clapham was still serving breakfast when Pat Harrison got out of bed, put on her dressing gown and went for a shower. Plummer sat up in bed and wished he was with her. Their night had been one of passionate lovemaking, far better than he had expected. Pat had surprised him by revealing her insatiable sexual appetite and now he wanted to experience another night with her. He was still feeling tired and rested his head on the pillow while he waited for her to leave the bathroom.

It was the knock on the door that woke him. He heard the sound of a vacuum cleaner and realized it was the girls arriving to clean the rooms. He looked at his watch and was surprised to see it read 10.15. He went to the door and asked the girl to come back later. It was then that he realized Pat had left the room without disturbing him. Then he saw that her bag had gone and looked around to see if she had left him a note but he found nothing. He took a quick shower then packed his bag and left the room, hoping that Pat might still be in the dining room that finished serving breakfast at 10 a.m. Unable to see her, he went to the receptionist and asked if Miss Harrison had left a message and was told she had checked out. He was now convinced that she had used him as he had used her, purely for sex, and he was angry. Then a young man, who was sitting at a desk in the corner of reception, looked up and asked, 'Are you Bob, sir?'

'Yes,' he replied.

'Miss Harrison wants you to call her on this number, sir.' The young man placed a piece of paper on the desk, at the same time explaining to the girl, 'You were in the back when she checked out, so she gave it to me.'

Plummer could see that it was a mobile phone number and was pleased Pat wanted to hear from him. He decided to make the call from a phone box so that his conversation was private. He got some change from the receptionist and left the hotel to find a telephone box. He finally found one that was free and went inside and dialled the number. He was annoyed to hear the engaged tone and, deciding to try again later, went to a café for some breakfast.

★ ★ ★

When WPC Barbara French arrived at the home of Mike Long, she was dressed in a two-piece suit. She rang the bell and had a file of papers in her hand. Mike opened the door and gave an enquiring look.

'Are you Michael Kenneth Long, known as Mike Long?'

'That's me, yes.'

'I'm from the Inland Revenue, Mr Long. I wonder if I could come in and check one or two things that are down on your tax return as expenses for business purposes. It will only take a few moments.' She could see that he had been caught off-guard.

'My accountant does my tax returns,' he said, looking slightly concerned.

'Nevertheless I would like to just see the suits, shoes, et cetera. Purely to satisfy my superiors that they do exist, you understand,' she said with a slight smile.

'Yes. Well. You'd better come in,' he said.

She went in and followed him to the bedroom, where he opened the doors of a large built-in wardrobe. It was full of very smart tailor-made suits that she counted, then checked a paper in her file as though ticking items. Without saying anything, she bent down to study the many pairs of shoes on a double rack and made notes of the ones she thought would be of interest to Inspector Forward. After looking at some shirts, she turned to leave.

'Thank you for your help, Mr Long. Everything seems to be in order.'

Mike Long was relieved as he showed her to the front door and watched her go.

★ ★ ★

Bob Plummer finished his breakfast and went back to the telephone box to try Pat's number again. He was pleased when she answered.

'Hello, Bob. You woke up, then.'

'Pat. What happened? Why did you go like that?'

'You were fast asleep and I had to hurry. My mobile rang and I was asked to bring my first appointment forward as the person I was meeting was catching an early flight. And as you were fast asleep I crept out without stopping for any breakfast.'

'I didn't hear your mobile ring,' Bob said.

'I had it on buzz so it didn't actually ring. In any case, I thought you needed a good rest after last night's activity. God, I've never met a man with your stamina before. You certainly know how to tire a girl out. But don't think that I'm complaining. Last night was an experience I shall not forget in a hurry. You're a great teacher, Bob.'

'So where will you be tonight?' he asked.

'I was planning to have an early dinner and catch up on my sleep. Why? Do you have another suggestion?'

'Yes. Why don't we have an early night together? Where are you staying?'

'I shall be at the Morgan Hotel in Lewisham. It's one of a chain that I get a special rate with. Shall we do what we did last night? Meet at 5.30 and have a drink before dinner?'

'That sounds good to me.'

89

'OK. I look forward to it.'

'Me too. I'll see you later.'

He was convinced Pat had sounded eager and excited at the prospect of another night together. He had time to kill before their meeting and although he wanted to find Sergeant Forward, he was aware that his photograph was circulating around the police, so he dare not risk being seen until he had changed his appearance again. But he knew he couldn't do this while he was seeing Pat as she only knew him as he was now — and he wouldn't do anything to destroy their relationship while his sex life was proving so successful. He decided to go to a cinema, where he could pass the afternoon in the dark and away from the eyes of the law.

★　★　★

WPC French reported back to Inspector Forward as soon as she returned to his office.

'So how did you get on?' Bill enquired.

'He's got more suits than Marks and Spencer. And I got a good look at the shoes too.'

'Were they there?'

'Yes, grey suede with brass fancy bits across the toes. Fairly new but they have been worn,' she said.

'Excellent. And how was he with the lady from the Inland Revenue?' Bill smiled.

'Not happy but I had to thank him for his help. It's like I said, sir, men like him are more scared of the tax man than the police. He looked relieved when I left.'

'Did you ask him where he was yesterday afternoon?' asked Marsh.

'No. I didn't want him to panic and get rid of what he was wearing.'

'Well, thank you, and well done, French.'

Marsh saw her out and turned to Bill. 'What do you want to do now? Bring him in for questioning?'

'Yes. And we shall bring those shoes in as well. I want the Father to see them and confirm that they are what he saw when he was attacked. Come on, Sergeant. Let's get a search warrant in case Mr Long is reluctant to give us the shoes.'

Marsh looked surprised. 'But WPC French could have taken them if she had wanted to. So why would he be reluctant to give them to us?'

'Because he thought she was from the Inland Revenue, whereas we are only policemen.' Bill grinned.

They left the office, Bill looking happier now that he was working from the police station again. Complete with a search warrant, he and Marsh set off for the home of Mike Long. Bill had forgotten about his armed protection officer until he saw Roberts' car pull in behind them and park. He then remembered Bob Plummer and was glad his wife Jane now had a policewoman looking after her.

Marsh rang the bell and Mike Long opened the door. He was wearing a very smart suit and some expensive-looking shoes. Bill Forward produced his warrant card. 'Michael Kenneth Long?'

'I am, yes,' he answered, looking puzzled.

'I am Detective Inspector Forward and this is Detective Sergeant Marsh. We have reason to believe that you could help us with our enquiries regarding an attack on a priest and would like you to accompany us to the station for further questioning.'

'I have no idea what you're talking about.'

'About the attack on a priest, that we believe you may have witnessed,' said Marsh.

'And we would like to take a pair of your shoes that we think may have been seen when the attack took place,' Bill explained.

Mike Long tried to hide his discomfort as he said, 'I shall call my solicitor, who will no doubt ask you to provide a search warrant before you take anything from my home.'

Bill took the search warrant from his

pocket and handed it to him. 'I think you will find this is in order. Where is your bedroom, sir?'

Long realized he had no choice but to show them. 'It's this way, gentlemen.' He led them to the bedroom and Marsh went to the wardrobe and opened the doors while Bill stood admiring the suits.

'You have some beautiful clothes, sir. I think I'm in the wrong job.'

Long forced a grateful smile as he watched Marsh looking at the vast shoe rack. But his smile vanished when he saw Marsh pick up the grey suede pair with the brass bits over the toes. Marsh held them up and showed them to Bill, who gave an affirmative nod.

'These look like the ones we want to take,' Bill told Mike Long. 'We believe they were seen by someone who can confirm that it was the pair the attacker was wearing as he struck the priest.'

'Are you accusing me of hitting a priest? What rubbish. I haven't worn those shoes for ages.'

Bill took Marsh to one side and gave him instructions. Marsh left, taking the shoes with him, and Mike Long was obviously worried.

'I would prefer to continue this at the police station, sir.'

'If you are intending to charge me with

anything I shall insist that my solicitor is there to advise me. I know my rights.'

'And what offence do you think I might be charging you with, Mr Long?' Bill asked.

'Hitting a priest, I believe you said.'

'I don't remember accusing you of that, sir. But as a matter of interest, do you mind telling me where you were yesterday morning?'

'I was in my office, working.'

'On a Sunday morning?'

'I have to work any day of the week, Inspector. I imagine you have to do the same.'

Bill nodded and said, 'That's true, sir, very true.'

'May I ask where your sergeant has gone with my shoes?'

'To see the person who saw them on the priest's attacker,' Bill said casually, hoping for a reaction from Mike Long.

'So someone saw them, then?' said Long.

'Oh yes, sir. After all, they are very unusual shoes, as I'm sure you will agree. Anyone seeing them would never forget them.'

'So someone else has those shoes,' Long said. 'I was sold them believing they were the only pair. It looks as if I was had, Inspector.' He smiled and gave a forlorn shrug. 'I don't suppose I would get my money back, though.

You know what those market traders are like.'

Bill listened patiently to him trying to squirm out of any suggestion that he could be the attacker.

'If you still want your solicitor present when we go to the station, I suggest you give him a call now and he can meet you there.'

Mike Long hesitated for a moment and then went to his phone and made a call. He got into Roberts' police car and wondered if this was some sort of set-up between the police and the woman from the Inland Revenue who had called on him earlier. He just hoped he would get a chance to speak with his solicitor in private before being interviewed.

7

DS Marsh arrived at the hospital, went to Father O'Connor's room and showed him the shoes. The priest didn't hesitate in his response.

'Yes, yes. They're the shoes I saw when I fell to the ground.'

'No doubt at all, Father?'

'No, none, Sergeant. My head is a lot clearer now and they are not shoes I will forget in a hurry, I can tell you. So have you arrested someone?'

'Inspector Forward will make a decision on that, once the man has been interviewed. I must get back to the station. He will want me there to tell him that you identified these shoes. He may want a written statement from you but he will let you know if he does. I'll be off now, Father.'

'Thank you for coming, Sergeant. Give the inspector my regards.'

'I will.'

Marsh hurried back to his car and called Bill to tell him Father O'Connor's reaction to seeing the shoes.

★   ★   ★

Mike Long was not in a good mood when he arrived at the police station as his solicitor was not there to meet him. He looked at his watch and became irritable and impatient.

'God knows I pay the man enough. You'd think he'd be here.'

'He's probably held up in the traffic, sir. Would you like a cup of coffee?' Bill asked.

'No, thank you. I need something stronger than coffee.'

Bill went to a coffee machine but changed his mind. He had never found that coffee as nice as the freshly made one from the canteen and decided to give it a miss. He sat with Long on a seat outside an interview room and hoped Marsh would soon get there so that he could start interviewing his suspect.

From where Long was sitting, he could see various police people going in and out. Some were in uniform, others in ordinary civilian clothes, and he began to get restless.

'How long do you intend keeping me here?'

Before Bill could answer, Marsh arrived. 'There we are, sir. He gave a positive ID on these. They were definitely the shoes worn by the attacker, he said.'

'Thank you, Sergeant. He's an important witness.'

'May I ask who this important witness is?' asked Long.

'Father O'Connor, sir.'

'The priest who was attacked?'

'Yes, sir.'

'But I thought he was knocked unconscious.'

'And who told you that, sir?'

'Well, I thought somebody said it,' Long said awkwardly.

'Let's go to the interview room. I think we've wasted enough of our time. This way, sir,' said Bill, indicating room number one.

'What about my solicitor?'

'Sergeant Cooper on the desk will show him in when he arrives,' said Marsh as he opened the door to the interview room. Mike Long entered the room and looked nervous.

'If you would sit there, sir, then your solicitor can sit next to you when he gets here,' said Bill.

Mike Long reluctantly went to one side of a long table while Bill and Marsh sat opposite.

'Now, sir, perhaps you can tell us what you were doing in Conway Street yesterday morning,' said Bill.

'I thought you had to wait for my solicitor to be present before asking me questions,' said Long. 'In any case, I don't even know a Conway Street.'

'It's the street where the Father was attacked and where your shoes were seen, Mr

Long,' said Marsh.

'As I said before, someone must have the same shoes as me, because I wasn't there.'

The door opened and Sergeant Cooper ushered John Hall into the room. 'This is Mr John Hall, solicitor.'

Hall had a face Bill recognized from a previous meeting with a local villain and he knew he was a shrewd man.

'I should like a few moments with my client before any official questioning takes place,' said Hall. 'And I trust no tape-recording has taken place prior to my arrival.'

'No. We haven't had the machine switched on as your client, I am sure, will verify.' Bill and Marsh got up to leave. 'Will five minutes be enough for you?' asked Bill.

Hall nodded. 'I'm sure it will, thank you, Inspector.'

As they left, Bill looked at his watch. 'Come on, Sergeant. We've got time for a coffee if we hurry.'

They got to the canteen and sat waiting for five minutes to pass when Marsh suddenly said, 'Don't you think we should find out what Benny Sutherland was doing in the area when Terry Kennedy saw him drive past the club?'

'Yes, I do. But we can do that after we've had a chat with Mike Long. Whichever way we do it, one of them is bound to tip the other one off that we are getting close to finding out who's responsible for the attack on Father O'Connor. Drug pushers are like fly paper — they always stick together. They are without doubt a nasty group of buggers.'

It was nearer ten minutes by the time they had finished their coffee and returned to the interview room.

John Hall was sitting beside Mike Long as Bill and Marsh entered the room — and was ready to earn his fee. 'Now that you have returned, my client wishes to make a statement.'

Bill was interested to hear what Mike Long had to say.

'I was not wearing the shoes you brought from my home, Inspector, not yesterday or any other day recently. So you see, either they were borrowed by someone without my knowledge or, as is more likely, they were identical shoes that were purchased from the same shoemaker by someone who was in the area at the time the priest was injured. A simple misunderstanding on your part, Inspector, as I think you will agree.'

Bill gave a wry smile and said, 'It was just a coincidence then. But have you any idea who it was that wanted to buy those identical shoes?'

'No idea.' Mike shrugged.

'But surely someone must have admired them and asked where you got them and how much they cost?' said Marsh.

'It could have been anyone. Everyone admires the way I dress.'

'Someone like Benny Sutherland, you mean?' asked Bill, as he and Marsh watched the look of discomfort between John Hall and his client.

'I don't think I'm familiar with that person, Inspector,' said Long, trying to sound convincing.

'Well, Mr Hall is. You represent him, don't you, sir?' said Bill, looking Hall in the eyes.

'He has called on my professional assistance in the past, yes. May I ask what that has to do with my client, Michael Long?'

Hall leaned in to Mike and whispered instructions to him.

'What made you ask about Benny Sutherland?' asked Mike.

'Because he was seen driving away from the Conway Street area around the time that Father O'Connor was attacked, sir.'

'I really think my client has been more than helpful. But we both know the law, Inspector. You must either charge my client or release him,' said Hall.

Bill raised an eyebrow and looked surprised. 'But your client is not under arrest, sir. He can leave whenever he wishes. But I would like to thank him for his willingness to help us with our enquiries. He has been most helpful.' He smiled.

Mike Long couldn't believe what the inspector was saying. 'But you insisted you brought me here rather than interview me at my home!'

'Yes, so that we could have our chat without telephones ringing and interrupting us, sir. We had no idea that you thought we were arresting you, did we, Sergeant?'

'Indeed not. That was the last thing on our mind, sir,' said Marsh convincingly.

John Hall got to his feet. 'Then we shall bid you goodbye, gentlemen.'

Hall opened the door and held it for Mike Long. As they left, Marsh smiled at Bill.

'I love the way you got their knickers in a twist. What do you think they'll do now?'

'The first thing Michael Long will do is realize he's left his shoes here. Then they will wonder what our next move will be.'

'And what will it be?'

'See if Sergeant Cooper has got an address for Benny. If he has, we'll get over there with the shoes and find out if he *has* a similar pair. One way or another, I intend to nail the man that attacked Father O'Connor.'

It was almost dusk when Bob Plummer left the cinema and boarded a bus for Lewisham. He went upstairs and sat at the back, picking up a discarded newspaper to read and help cover his face from prying eyes. He was determined to alter his appearance tomorrow and was wondering what style and colour he should have. Just then two teenagers got up from their seats and the ludicrous hairstyles they had chosen made him smile. He would need something more adult and less notice-able than blue and red striped pieces of hair in a Mohican-style cut. He looked at his watch and knew that within the hour he would be alone with Pat, and that thought began stirring his sexual feelings again. He decided she was more important to think about than a change of hairstyle.

When Bill and Marsh arrived at Benny Sutherland's house, they saw his car parked there.

'Well, there's his car, so with a bit of luck he's in,' Bill said as they stopped. 'Let's see what he has to say for himself.'

They went to the front door and Marsh

stood back with the shoes while Bill rang the doorbell. Benny's wife Marion opened the door and Bill produced his warrant card.

'I'm DI Forward and this is DS Marsh. We would like a word with Benny, please.'

'I don't know if he's in.'

'Oh, I think you will find he is,' said Bill, smiling. 'May we step inside or would you rather we spoke to him out here?'

Marion knew better than to antagonize the police and stepped back for them to enter the hall. 'I'll give him a call.'

Bill and Marsh waited a moment and could hear voices in the distance. Benny appeared from a back room and gave his visitors a smile.

'You wanted to see me, gentlemen?'

'Yes. I'm — '

'Marion told me who you were. What can I do for you?'

Marsh took the shoes from the bag. 'Are these your shoes, sir?' asked Marsh.

Benny looked at them and laughed. 'I wouldn't be seen wearing those! What made you think they were mine?'

'A priest was attacked in Conway Street yesterday and his attacker was wearing shoes like these,' said Bill.

'What's that got to do with me?' asked Benny.

'You were seen driving away from that area,' said Marsh.

'And you think I attacked a priest just because I might have been driving round that area? I often drive through that way but I don't know anything about a priest.'

'Then why did you enquire about him at the hospital?'

'Who told you that? They must have got me muddled up with somebody else.'

'Oh no, Mr Sutherland, I saw you there myself. You were asking if you could see him. Now why would you be asking to see a priest who you knew nothing about?' asked Bill.

'Now hang on,' he said, pretending to remember. 'You mean the old man who runs a boys' club? Oh yes — when I heard he had been injured I went to see how he was. They say he does a lot to keep the boys off the streets. I'd nearly forgotten about *him*. He's going to be all right, isn't he?' he asked, as if he was concerned.

'Yes. He'll be up and about in no time,' said Marsh.

'Getting back to the shoes, Mr Sutherland, have you any idea who might own such a pair?'

Benny shook his head. 'No.'

'Someone like Mike Long, for instance,' said Bill. 'He's the tall man with a very expensive wardrobe in case you can't place him. And like you, he is an admirer of the boys' club that Father O'Connor runs. And like you, he was upset to think that anyone could be evil enough to attack a priest.'

'I might know him if I saw him. What sort of business is he in?'

'Officially he runs an agency for house sitters. But that's really his wife's business. I think he makes his extra cash doing the same as you do. You should get together. Come on, Sergeant. I think we've taken up enough of this man's time. Thanks for your help, Mr Sutherland.'

'I don't think I've been much help really, Inspector.'

'Oh, but you have, sir. More than you know.'

Bill and Marsh left the house and got into the car. 'His face was a picture when you said he was more of a help than he knew. Now he'll be trying to work out what he said that might have helped us.' Marsh smiled. 'I wonder how much honour there really is among thieves?'

'People like him and Mike Long don't know the meaning of the word honour. I think it's a good time for Terry Kennedy to switch on his biro and have a chat with his friend Ronnie Hicks. Then with luck we shouldn't have too long to wait before we hear him say who *his* supplier is.'

'But Terry picked out Benny Sutherland from the mugshots of the man he saw offering the boys — how did he put it? — 'something to make you feel a lot better'.'

'That's true. But I want to hear it from Ronnie himself. I shall give Terry a call and try and set it up. Then I shall give Dave Norris a call and let him know what I'm doing.'

8

Pat Harrison had been to the bathroom and changed into a dress that she thought would appeal to Bob. She stood in front of the full-length mirror of the wardrobe door and was happy with her appearance. The low-cut neck showed just enough cleavage to excite but wasn't too provocative. She wanted to have drinks and dinner before letting Bob get her into bed. And tonight she wanted him to be a little more rough and demanding with his foreplay. The thought of him slapping her and ordering her to do what he wanted made her feel very excited. Bob knew how to satisfy her more than other men she had met recently. He was a man she wanted to experiment with and try things that were more adventurous. She sat on the edge of the bed, looking at the two glasses she had waiting for the after-dinner drinks they would have before indulging in sex. She looked at her watch and knew that he would soon be knocking on her door and hoped she was able to hide the excitement his arrival gave her. She was wondering what new things she would experience with him tonight. She didn't have to wait long before there was a knock. She quickly checked her appearance and opened the door. The man standing there was not Bob. He was full of apologies as he introduced himself.

'Sorry to bother you, miss. I'm the caretaker and would like to check your hot water if I may. Some of the guests are complaining that it's coming through cold. I shall not keep you long.' He walked to the bathroom.

'I showered a short time ago and it was hot enough then,' Pat told him. He mumbled something in reply but the phone rang and she didn't hear what he said. She picked up the phone and heard Bob's voice.

'Hello, Pat. The charming girl at reception tells me you've got a man up there. Is it safe to come up?' he joked.

'It's the caretaker,' she whispered. 'So while he's hiding in the bathroom I'll sneak out and meet you in the bar.'

'Good idea. I'll order the drinks. Gin and tonic for you?'

'Yes, please. I'm on my way.'

She told the caretaker that she was leaving and left the room. When she got to the bar, Bob was taking the drinks to a table in an alcove. She smiled as she approached him.

'Hello, stranger,' she said.

Bob put the drinks down and kissed her cheek. As he did so, he moved his lips to her ear. 'God, I wish we were in your room, lovely lady,' he whispered.

'After dinner, you *will* be, randy man.' They sat down opposite each other and raised their glasses. 'Cheers. I really am glad you came. I've thought about you quite a lot.'

'I thought about you too. You're one hell of an exciting woman, you know.'

'I'm glad you find me so. I don't understand how you're a free man. I would have thought a woman would have tried to hook you long before now.'

'Just call me lucky.' He smiled.

'But if and when one does, what will she be changing her name to?'

He was prepared for her to ask what his surname was and answered without hesitation. 'Wilson. It was the name of our prime minister a few years ago. A good thing it wasn't Blair. *Blair* sounds like someone throwing up,' he said with a chuckle.

'Yes, I prefer Wilson.' Pat smiled.

They sat in silence for a while and then Bob put his hand under the table and rested it on her knee. As he started to stroke it, he felt her hand touching his leg and giving him a squeeze of encouragement. Bob was becoming frustrated and tried to put her hand on his thigh. Suddenly she took her hand away as she saw the caretaker at the bar door. He saw Pat and signalled that everything was all right in her room. Bob saw her acknowledge someone and turned round to see who it was.

'It was the caretaker to tell me he's finished in my room.'

Bob made no effort to hide the fact that he wanted to get her to bed and said, 'Let's go and see if he did a good job.'

Pat nodded. 'I'll tell the dining room we shall be in later.' She took his arm and went to the receptionist. 'Mr Wilson and I will eat later. We have some paperwork we need to go through before we eat. You will tell them, won't you?'

'Yes, of course, miss.'

When they arrived at the bedroom, Pat removed the Do Not Disturb sign from inside the door and hung it on the outside handle. As she closed the door she said, 'Mustn't be disturbed while we're going through our paperwork.' She then pulled the bed cover off and sat on the bed with her back to Bob. 'Unzip me.' Her voice was soft and she spoke with a tremble. 'Then you can take your things off.

Bob pulled her zip down and as she took off her dress he took off his shirt, trousers and underwear and threw them on to a chair. He took her in his arms and as they kissed each other passionately he moved a hand to her bra and unhooked it. As he caressed and kissed her breast, she became more excited and frustrated. Unable to control her feelings, she pushed his hand down until it was inside her panties. As he began to massage her, she became more and more breathless with excitement. He wanted to give her an orgasm and because he was getting close to one himself, he moved her hand to his genitals for her to masturbate him. Within moments they both reached a climax. They were exhausted and lay motionless for a while.

'Oh, Bob. You really are incredible.'

'You're pretty wonderful yourself.'

'Now we have a choice. Shower or sleep for a while.'

'Stay here and give dinner a miss, you mean?'

'You'll need to feed that body of yours because I want you to have the strength to give a repeat performance later,' Pat said as she gave his cheek a gentle kiss.

'In that case, shall I shower first or will you?' asked Bob with a cheeky smile.

'We mustn't waste water. Why not shower together?'

'I may have to rape you if we do.'

'In that case I shall scream for the caretaker.'

They both laughed and then Bob used the moment to mention his intended change of appearance.

'By the way, Pat.'

'Yes?'

'I want your opinion on something. I've got to trace a man who might recognize me unless I make one or two changes to my appearance. My hair, for instance. What colour would suit me, do you think?'

After studying his hair for a moment she said, 'Auburn. I think you would look nice with auburn hair.'

'Yes, I like that. I was thinking of making my moustache thinner and perhaps grow a goatee beard like the French have.'

'Oh yes, I would like that. Then you could make love to me and tell me in a French accent what you want to do.' She stroked his thigh and could feel him getting aroused again. In a sexy whisper she asked, 'Would you do that for me?'

His breathing became more rapid as he closed his eyes and lay back, enjoying the way she was fondling him. 'You keep doing that and I'll show you what I want.'

As though giving an order she said, 'Show me what you want, Bob. Show me.'

He pulled her over so that she was on top of him. He was hard now and she had no trouble guiding him into her. His hands were holding her bottom and as he thrust himself further inside her, he could feel one of her breasts touching him. She moved it closer to his mouth.

'Suck me, Bob, suck me,' she instructed him.

As he began sucking her, he gently bit her nipple and this excited her. They were working each other towards another climax and within a few moments Bob was having an orgasm. Pat was close to reaching a climax and pleaded, 'Don't stop. Oh God. Yes. Yes!' Soon they had both felt total satisfaction and the two of them lay beside each other, exhausted again.

'Can you imagine how we would be if we were together all the time?' she said.

Bob smiled and said, 'We would probably kill each other by overindulging in sex.'

'That's true, but what a wonderful way to go. I need that shower now. Coming?'

'I thought I just had,' he replied with a cheeky grin.

She kissed him and got off the bed. 'Well, I don't want to kill you just yet, so you lie there and get your strength back.' As she walked towards the bathroom she turned and added,

'You'll need it for later.'

'Is that a threat or a promise?' he asked.

'You'll have to wait and see, won't you?' she said, smiling.

As she went to shower he wished the police were not looking for him and that he was free to be seen out with her. He decided he would change his appearance tomorrow and then he could do whatever he wanted without anyone interfering.

★ ★ ★

Terry Kennedy arrived at the club with his biro pen placed in his top pocket, exactly as Dave Norris had instructed. He was slightly nervous as he approached Ronnie Hicks, who was pacing anxiously up and down outside.

'Hi, Ronnie, are you OK?'

'Fine. Has anyone been here looking for me?'

'I don't know. Who are you expecting?'

Ronnie sounded anxious. 'Just someone who promised to bring something for me, that's all. I hope he hasn't got the days mixed up.'

'You need what he was bringing, do you?'

'Yes, I do.'

Terry wanted Ronnie to say something positive for his recorder to pick up and asked,

'Is there anything I can help you with?'

'I doubt it.'

'Try me.'

'I don't think you sell what I want, Terry.'

'You mean a powder that makes you feel better?'

Ronnie suddenly brightened up. 'Yeah, yeah, have you got some?'

Terry pretended he was trying to remember. 'He wanted me to have some. Now what was his name? Something like Kenny, it was.'

'Was he a smartly dressed man?'

'Yes, that's him.'

'That's Benny.'

'So that's who you're waiting for and he's got powder for you, has he, Ronnie? Sorry I can't help.'

'You're not on it, then?'

'No. I didn't want to get reliant on that stuff. You can do without it, surely. It can't be nice having to sniff powder up your nose in order to feel good.'

'It's horrible being without it. But once you take it you feel really great.'

'Are any of the other boys on it?' Terry asked.

'I don't know.' Ronnie became more restless and began to sweat.

'Only if they were, they might be able to give you some of their powder. Until Benny turns up, I mean. You can't go on like this. Either you're becoming an addict and need help or you'll end up a junkie somewhere. Ronnie, you must talk to Father O'Connor. I'm sure he will help you.'

Ronnie's mouth was dry and he began shaking slightly. 'I don't think he'd approve of me taking coke. He might even kick me out of the club.'

'You know him better than that. He wouldn't like the idea of that Benny trying to get the boys hooked, that's for sure. By the way, how much does he charge you for the stuff?'

'The first lot was a free sample.'

'Why did you take it? You must have known it was a drug he was giving you.'

'He said it would make me feel great and it did. I couldn't describe what it's like, Terry. It was fabulous and it was free.'

'But you don't feel fabulous now, do you? That's the curse of drugs. Once you're hooked, you're hooked. What does it cost you now?'

'The last lot was £10 but he said this time it will be more because the price of coke has gone up.'

'And it will go up again. So where will you get the money from?'

Ronnie knew Terry was right and kept

117

rubbing his head nervously. 'What am I going to do, Terry?'

'Let's go inside and sit down and you can have a strong black coffee. And then I shall phone a friend of mine who might know what to do. Come on.'

Terry placed a friendly hand on Ronnie's shoulder and they walked into the club.

★   ★   ★

Bill Forward telephoned Dave Norris on his mobile. 'I just had a call from Terry Kennedy. He's been chatting to the Hicks lad with his biro recorder switched on.'

'And?'

'It's as we thought, Dave. The pusher is Benny Sutherland and the boy was waiting for a new supply from him when Terry got to the club. Apparently Ronnie Hicks is getting withdrawal symptoms because Benny hadn't turned up as he had promised to.'

'Are they at the club now?'

'Yes.'

'I'll ring Terry and tell him what to do. Leave it with me.' He hung up and rang Terry from the car. 'Hello, Terry, this is Inspector Norris. Inspector Forward told me you got your friend Ronnie to name Benny Sutherland.'

'That's right.'

'Good lad. Now listen, I want you to tell Ronnie that Benny won't be coming and that a friend of yours will pick him up in fifteen minutes and is going to help him.'

'OK.'

'Let him think I'm going to supply his needs if he wants to but don't tell him who I am. Just that I'm a friend. Do you understand?'

'Yes, understood.'

'Good lad.'

When he'd finished the call, Terry went back to Ronnie and said, 'That was a friend of mine. He said Benny won't be coming tonight but that he will be here in about fifteen minutes to pick you up. He said he will help you. You can survive another fifteen minutes, can't you?'

Ronnie nodded. 'Going to bring something for me, is he?'

'I don't know but he's a nice man, you can trust him.'

Ronnie looked at his watch and became restless. 'Your friend won't be long, will he?'

'He'll be here soon. Try and relax. Have another coffee.' Terry got him a coffee and sat with him, hoping Inspector Norris wouldn't be too long.

'Have you known this man long?' Ronnie

asked. 'I mean, how do you know you can trust him?'

'I've known him long enough to know he can be trusted. I would trust him with my life. Now, does that put your mind at rest?'

Ronnie managed a smile and nodded. Then he sipped his coffee and tried to control his hand from shaking too much as he drank. Just over ten minutes had passed when Dave Norris arrived but it had seemed like an eternity to Ronnie, who was sweating and shaking more than ever. Dave gave them a wave and they followed him outside. He opened the front passenger door for Ronnie to get in. While Ronnie was doing so, Terry quickly passed the biro to Dave, who got in the driver's seat and pulled away.

'I thought we would drive and have a chat away from the club, Ronnie.'

'Have you got some stuff for me?' Ronnie asked hopefully.

'I thought Benny Sutherland was your supplier.'

'He never turned up today like he said he would.'

'That's because the police are on to him which means he won't worry about anyone other than himself. As long as he's trying to save his own neck, he won't bother about you, Ronnie, you can be certain of that.'

'But I need a fix and Terry said you were a friend who can help me.'

'And I want to, believe me. But not in the way you think.' He quietly pressed the door-lock control to prevent Ronnie getting out and making a run for it.

'I don't understand. How do you mean, you can help me?'

'I can put you in touch with a man who would stop you being dependent on drugs and, as you have only been on cocaine a short while, he'll have your system clean and back to normal in no time. Just think, Ronnie, no more paying people like Benny for drugs that will end up killing you.'

Ronnie was obviously confused as he asked, 'Are you a doctor? I thought you were going to give me a fix but I don't even know who you are.'

'I'm a friend of Terry's who wants to help you. With a bit of luck, Benny won't be supplying drugs for a long time. But someone else will come in his place and you will end up paying more and more until you don't have enough money left. Then you will start stealing to get the money you'll need to satisfy your craving. And because you will have become a junkie and a thief, you'll eventually go to prison and spend years locked up with other criminals. Is that what you want?'

121

Ronnie shook his head. 'No! I just want to feel better.'

'Then let me take you to someone who will do that. Who do you live with Ronnie? Your parents?'

'Yes.'

'Do they know about your problem?'

'No!' Ronnie shouted. 'They'd kill me if they knew.'

'But if Father O'Connor arranged a few days away for you on one of his club outings, they would agree to that, would they?'

'Yes. But if he knew I was taking drugs he'd be horrified. He'd never forgive me.'

'You underestimate the man, Ronnie. He would do all he could to help, you know that. One quick phone call and I can arrange it. Shall I do it?'

'But I would have to go home to get my things and my dad would know I was taking drugs. He'd go mad.'

'It can be arranged so that you won't have to go home. I'll ring a friend of mine who can make sure no-one, not even your parents, know. Trust me.' Dave pulled into a parking bay and called Bill Forward, careful not to let Ronnie know he was talking to a police officer. 'It's Dave. I've got the lad from the boys' club in the car with me.'

'How is he?' asked Bill.

'He's going to be fine. He's agreed to go to my friend's clinic, so he will be away for a few days, and I wonder if you would do something for me.'

'If I can, of course I will.'

'Get Father O'Connor to call on his parents and collect the few things the lad will need. Washing things, pyjamas and a change of underwear et cetera, and get the Father to tell his parents he is going away on an adventure trip for a few days. It's a chance-in-a-lifetime thing. He'll know what to say.'

'There's just one slight problem with that idea, Dave.'

'What's that?'

'Father O'Connor isn't coming out of hospital until the morning, so he wouldn't be able to get the boys' things till then.'

Dave thought carefully and then said, 'OK. Get Terry to go and collect them. They'll trust him and he can tell them the Father will phone them.' Dave turned to Ronnie and asked, 'You are on the phone at home, I take it?'

'Yes. Terry and Father O'Connor know our number.'

'Good. It's OK Bill. Get the Father to call the parents and tell them about the trip he's arranged for Ronnie and that Terry is calling round for their son's things. Terry can tell them he's envious but there was only one place going and that Ronnie's got it. Then get his things over to me at the clinic. I'll give Terry a call and tell him what I want him to do.'

'OK Dave. I'll get Father O'Connor to phone Ronnie's home from the hospital right away.'

Within minutes the calls were made and everything was set up for Ronnie to go into the clinic and dry out.

9

Pat Harrison was awoken by her alarm buzzing. She looked at the time through bleary eyes and wished she could turn over and go back to sleep. But her appointment was just over an hour and a half away and it would take her that long to shower, dress and get to the client, so there was no time for more sleep. She looked at Bob, who was conscious of her moving and opened one eye.

'Oh God, are you going to get up now?' he asked.

'Yes. I wish I could stay but I've got a job to do.'

'Yes, of course you have. Come to think of it, so have I.' He took her hand and held it as he said, 'You were terrific last night, Pat. I reckon we get better together, don't you?'

'Well, you do, that's for sure.' She leant down to kiss him. 'Ouch. You've got a prickly beard.'

'I know, sorry. That's the job I've got to do. Let it grow until it can be shaped into a goatee beard. Then I can get my hair dyed auburn for you.'

'How long will that take?'

'My hair grows very quickly so I could have

it all done in under a week. So the next time we meet I can be your new French lover.'

'What makes you think I can wait that long for another session with you? I don't mind getting pricked now and then as long as it's you doing the pricking.' She kissed his forehead and got up, leaving him feeling frustrated. As he waited for her to finish in the bathroom, he hoped it wouldn't be too long before he spent another night with her.

* * *

Superintendent Lamb called Inspector Forward to see him in his office and Bill went, wondering what it was about.

'Come in, Forward, and sit down. I've got some news for you regarding Bob Plummer.'

'Caught him, have they?' Bill asked hopefully.

'Not yet but I think we might be getting closer to him. A PC took Plummer's photograph to hotels in the Clapham area and a receptionist at the Morgan recognized him as a man who spent the night with a Miss Patricia Harrison.'

'When was that?'

'The night before last and the man's name was Bob. And when the Harrison woman checked out she left a phone number for him to reach her on.'

'Have they still got the number?'

'No. But the address she gave was care of a solicitors firm.' He pushed a piece of paper to Bill. 'That's their phone number. I thought you would like to give them a call. But be careful. Don't let them know you're a policeman in case they tell her and then Plummer would know we're on to him.'

'Don't worry, sir, I'll be discreet. I'll get on to this right away.'

'Good luck, Forward.'

'Thank you, sir.'

Bill left Lamb's office and hurried to his own. He sat down at his desk just as Marsh walked in with two mugs of coffee.

'You must be telepathic, Marsh. I was just thinking how welcome a coffee would be and here you are with it.'

'Well, it wasn't really telepathy on my part. I fancied one myself and it's more than my job's worth not to bring you one as well.'

'That's very wise, Marsh. A little thing like that could have you back in uniform and on the beat in no time.'

'You mean I'd have to bend my knees and look like a real policeman?'

'I'm afraid so. But only if you forget my coffee.'

Marsh smiled and asked, 'What did the super want?'

'He'd found out that Plummer stayed with a woman at the Morgan Hotel in Clapham two nights ago.'

'Who was the woman?'

'She checked in as Patricia Harrison, and gave a firm of solicitors as her address. I want to talk to the lady but I don't want her to know I'm a police officer in case she tells Plummer we're on to him.'

'Wait a minute. If she gave the solicitors as her address she might be a solicitor working with them, in which case she will have a mobile with her. Ring them and say you need to speak to her but have lost her number. They might even tell you where she is.'

'But talking to this woman isn't what bothers me. It's my getting her to tell me where Plummer is, if she knows.'

'Why not give the solicitors a call first? You know the old saying: 'Slowly, slowly, catchy monkey.''

'With your knowledge of Chinese proverbs, I'm surprised you didn't get transferred to London's Chinatown instead of Chelsea, Marsh. And now you can call the solicitors and get this woman's contact number for me. But don't speak in Cantonese, try English.'

Marsh ignored Bill's sarcasm and dialled the number Bill passed to him.

'Is that Belling and Musgrove?'

'It is.'

'I wonder if you can help me. I need to make contact with Patricia Harrison on a personal matter but I've lost her mobile phone number. Do you have it there?'

'A personal matter, you say?'

'Yes. It's important that I speak to her.'

'She will have left her hotel by now to call on a client but she switches her mobile off when she has a meeting with someone. She'll be at her hotel in Edgware this afternoon. She will be checking in after lunch and getting her papers ready for the meeting tomorrow morning. You could always reach her there. It's the Morgan Hotel.'

'Thank you for your help,' said Marsh and hung up.

Bill had watched him making notes and was impressed at the way Marsh had handled the call. 'Well, what did they say?'

'She is staying at the Morgan Hotel, Edgware tonight and will be there after lunch. Apparently she gets there so that she can get her paperwork sorted out for her meetings in the morning. They didn't say what she did but whether she is a solicitor or not, at least we know where she is today.'

Bill became thoughtful and said, 'And I wonder if there's a Morgan Hotel in Lewisham? If there is, that's probably where she stayed last night and who knows, even our friend Bob Plummer might have been with her.' He took a Yellow Pages from the shelf and thumbed through it. 'Bingo! I was right. Go down there and see if they recognize the photograph of Plummer. If they do, there's a good chance he'll be with her again tonight at the hotel in Edgware. Wouldn't it be lovely to nick him just as he was feeling lucky in a lady's boudoir?' Bill grinned.

'It would be lovely to nick him wherever he was. Have you got the photograph there?'

Bill took the picture from his drawer and gave it to Marsh. 'Be careful, in case he's still there. And good luck.'

★   ★   ★

It was just after 11.30 when Marsh arrived in Lewisham in south-east London. He parked at the Morgan Hotel and went to the receptionist with the photograph of Plummer.

'Excuse me. Can you tell me, is this gentleman staying in the hotel?'

The girl looked at the photograph and without hesitation said. 'I'm afraid you have missed him, sir. Mr Wilson left about half an hour ago.'

'Wilson? Are you sure that was his name?'

'Yes, sir. When Miss Harrison checked out

130

she said that Mr Wilson would be checking out later. Is something wrong, sir?'

'No, nothing. I just wanted to make sure we were talking about the man that stayed with her last night.'

'Oh yes, that's definitely the man she had with her on this visit. We just turn a blind eye to it these days. Being a hotel, we get used to it. Mind you, she is an attractive lady so you can't blame the men, I suppose.' Marsh was pleased the girl was so willing to talk about the infidelity of the guests.

'I imagine the chambermaids can tell a few stories, eh?' he said, smiling.

'You don't know the half of it,' she replied with a grin.

'Well, thank you. You have been most informative,' said Marsh.

'I hope what I told you won't get the lady into trouble. Only she's a regular here and I wouldn't want to cause her any bother,' said the receptionist. 'I could lose my job if they thought I was talking about the guests' private lives.'

'Don't worry. What you told me will be our secret.' Marsh gave her a wink and left to get into his car, where he called his boss and gave him an update.

'So my hunch was right about them staying together at the Morgan in Lewisham,' said Bill.

'Yes, and tonight she's at the one in Edgware. If he's with her there, we've got him.'

'You get back here, Marsh. I'll tell the super what you found out and see if he can arrange with Edgware to get a man at the hotel just in case our friend Plummer does turn up.'

★　★　★

Dave Norris played Bill the recording the biro pen had made. 'You see how clear it is, Bill. Young Terry was just the right distance from Ronnie when this was made.'

'I told you Terry was a reliable lad. So what's your next move?'

'We can pull Benny in and question him. But he would have his solicitor with him and he'd be sprung before we could do anything. We only have Ronnie telling Terry he was waiting for a fix from Benny, and that isn't enough to hold him on, as you know. What we really want is to get a bug on his telephone then we might learn where his next drop is going to be. Then we *would* have him. But as you know, it isn't easy getting permission to bug a phone.'

'I know it isn't politically correct to do so today, Dave, especially if the people are villains. God, remember the way we used to get results in the good old days when we could be proper coppers?' said Bill, smiling.

Dave nodded in agreement. 'Now we have to stick to the rules and get the paperwork in on time,' he sighed. 'Never mind, we can still get Benny and his chums put away if we play our cards right.'

'So what do you want to do?' asked Bill.

'The way I see it, we've only got two options. We can either wait for the Hicks lad to come out of the clinic and give him a wire and let him talk to Benny. Or give Terry another biro and let him go to Benny and pretend he's tried coke and likes it but wants to get more.'

Bill wasn't happy. 'Then what?'

'Keep our fingers crossed that we hear Benny talk himself into a long jail sentence.'

The expression on Bill's face told Dave he was not in favour of that. 'I know Terry is bright and reliable but I don't like the idea of him ending up in a hospital because we used him to get an arrest. These bastards are evil. Ask our friend Father O'Connor. Sorry, Dave, there has to be another way to trap Benny Sutherland without putting Terry's life at risk.'

Dave was obviously disappointed. 'Then we'll have to wait until the Hicks lad comes out of the clinic.'

10

Bob Plummer was pleased with his reflection in the mirror. His hair had dried a natural auburn colour but now he had to wait until his facial hair had grown before attempting to put dye on it. Then he would trim his moustache and cut his beard into shape. Once his appearance had changed, he would feel safe to leave the bedsit he had rented and enjoy the freedom of going out. Then he would be able to meet Pat whenever he wanted. And then he could find a certain policeman and enjoy the revenge he had promised himself. But he remembered Joe Levin's warning: 'Do that and you will spend the rest of your life behind bars.' Being behind bars again was the last thing he wanted. He didn't want to jeopardize his freedom by making a stupid mistake. He would have to find another way to make the policeman suffer. It was while he was reading a newspaper that he thought of the perfect way to do it. It would need cunning but if he was careful, his police adversary would suffer for the rest of his life. With Pat's help, Bob Plummer knew that he could satisfy his longing for vengeance. First, he would need to use her laptop and then he had to learn the whereabouts of the policeman. He went to the telephone in the hall and picked up the Yellow Pages to find the number of the Hackney police. Putting his coins in the phone box, he dialled the number and a female voice answered.

'Hackney police, can I help you?'

'I want to send a letter to my old friend, Sergeant Forward. Is he still stationed there at Hackney?'

'No. He's Detective Inspector Forward now and stationed at Chelsea.'

'Thank you very much.' Bob hung up, surprised at how easy it had been to discover Forward's whereabouts.

★ ★ ★

Dave Norris got in touch with the clinic and discovered that Ronnie Hicks was responding well to the treatment. He was told that Hicks could be out and back home again in about four weeks if his progress continued. Dave wasn't happy at having to wait that long and after he had finished his call he turned to Bill.

'They said Hicks is doing well.'

'That's good news.'

'But here's the bad news. He won't be out for at least another month. That's a waste of valuable time when we could trap these pushers and put them away. Why don't you let Terry do as I suggested?'

'Like I said, I don't want him ending up in hospital or a mortuary. People like Benny and Mike Long won't hesitate to get revenge if they think Terry has tricked them.'

Dave gave a shrug of acceptance. 'OK.' He got up and said goodbye to Bill and Marsh, then left to go back to his own office.

'I feel sorry for him in a way, but I agree with you as far as Terry is concerned,' said Marsh.

'Thank you, Sergeant, but now there's something else that worries me.'

'What's that, sir?'

'When you agree with me I get a shiver down my spine in case you're looking for promotion. And if you were to get promoted you would have to leave me and the thought of that makes me want to burst into tears. So before you go, will you give me an honest answer to a question?'

'Of course I will. What do you want to know?'

'Is there any chance of getting me a coffee?'

Marsh smiled to himself as he left the office for the canteen.

* * *

The following day was quieter than usual and Bill was hoping to get home early when his telephone rang. It was Superintendent Lamb.

'I'm glad I've caught you in, Forward. Come to my office before you go. I need to speak to you.'

'I'll come right away, sir.' He hung up. 'It's the super. I wonder what *he* wants?'

He walked past Marsh and down the corridor to Lamb's office.

'Come in, Forward. Take a seat. I thought we should discuss the threat that Plummer made and see where we go from here. I heard from my colleague in Edgware but he didn't turn up there last night. I take it you haven't had any kind of contact?'

'I haven't seen or heard from him since we knew about his threat to me. So I honestly don't know what is going on in his mind. I must say I do feel awkward having Roberts or Walker watching me all the time. I just want Plummer to show his face so we can get it over with.'

Lamb nodded in agreement. 'And now we have a WPC keeping an eye on your wife when you are out of the house. That's three people I've got tied up because of Plummer's threat to you. And no new sighting of him has been made so we have no idea what he looks like now.'

'We know he dyed his hair brown and grew a moustache.'

'Yes, but has he changed his appearance again?'

'I've wondered about that. And if he has we won't know *who* we are looking for,' Bill said with frustration.

'Well, I can keep the three officers protecting you for the time being, but not indefinitely. So let's hope he comes out of the woodwork soon.'

'Yes, let's hope he does. Goodnight, sir.'

Bill returned to his office feeling embarrassed that he was responsible for the upheaval the case was causing Lamb. As he went to his desk, Marsh gave an enquiring look.

'Is there a problem?'

'Yes, and I'm causing it in a way.'

'How do you mean?'

'The super's got three constables protecting Jane and I, all because of Plummer's threat to me. But he was only seen by Joe Levin and the receptionist in the hotels in Clapham and Lewisham, as far as we know. So why doesn't he find me? What the hell is he playing at?'

* * *

138

Jane Forward was in the sitting room with WPC Ruth Cunningham. The two women were talking about the price of food, clothes and the value of money generally as compared with last year. Jane had avoided talking about police business until now. But when Ruth mentioned that her husband had been a policeman, she was curious.

'You mean your husband *was* a policeman?'

'Yes. Up till two years ago he was with the riot squad. But he was in that Marsden street riot and got hit in the leg by a homemade bottle-bomb. The glass shattered and made a mess of his leg and left him with a limp. He was offered a desk job, so he still feels he is involved with police work, but not doing what he calls a proper policeman's job.'

'I can understand that. I don't think my husband would be happy if he had to sit at a desk all day,' said Jane.

'Who is this man Plummer? And why is he a danger to you and your husband?' asked Ruth.

'He's a man my husband arrested quite a while back. He had beaten his wife so violently that the poor woman had to endure plastic surgery. When he came to court it was my husband's evidence that got him put away and this man swore revenge on him.'

'Well, the superintendent obviously takes the threat seriously, otherwise I wouldn't be here.'

'It seems there was a constable involved in the arrest and he was badly beaten up by this Plummer. That's why we all have to take it seriously and hope he can be arrested again soon,' said Jane.

'Well, if he comes here he won't get far, I promise.' She gave the holster, holding her gun, a friendly pat.

Jane had never seen a woman from the protection squad before and the sight of her firearm being treated like a pet made her feel uncomfortable. She had been a policeman's wife for many years but even though times were changing, she was glad her husband didn't have to carry a gun. She just wanted to hear that Plummer had been caught so that she could get back to a normal life again.

★ ★ ★

Woman police sergeant Sally Hamilton rang Marsh's phone to delay their planned dinner together.

'Sorry, Dick. I have just been called to go and sort out a domestic that's come in, so I have no idea when I'll get back. Keep something warm for me. See you later.'

'OK.' Marsh hung up and looked at Bill. 'Sally's been called out to a domestic so she may not be back till late. I don't like it when she goes to sort out a domestic row. It doesn't matter which side is in the wrong, she has to act more like a counsellor than a police officer. Sometimes that can be a problem, especially if one of them gets violent.'

'Well, let's hope the man in this domestic quarrel isn't another Bob Plummer,' said Bill.

'Oh, don't. I couldn't bear it if anything nasty happened to Sally.' Marsh shivered at the thought.

Bill wished he hadn't mentioned Plummer and quickly changed the subject. 'I take it you're thinking of a future with this girl?'

'We've not discussed marriage, if that's what you mean.'

'But you must have thought about it. You can't spend a lot of time alone with a lovely girl like her and not have thought about it. I have a reason for asking you, Marsh.'

'And what's that, sir?'

'Well, if you do ask her and she says yes, don't have an engagement party.'

'Why?'

'Because then I would have to buy you an engagement present *and* a wedding present. And if I've retired I shall only have my pension so I couldn't afford both, could I?'

'There is an answer to that problem, sir.'

'And what's that?

'Don't retire,' Marsh said with a grin.

'Only on condition that you won't apply for promotion before I *do* retire. I'm getting too old to break in another young sergeant,' said Bill with a straight face.

'Break in? I'm not a racehorse.'

'Don't be modest. I bet you are quite a stallion when the mood takes you.'

Marsh was quietly amused but didn't reply, knowing that he couldn't win in an exchange of banter with DI Forward. And at the moment, Sally's safety was the main thing on his mind.

11

The constable on duty outside Father O'Connor's room at the hospital was the last person Bill expected to hear from when he picked up his telephone.

'This is Constable Warner, sir. Father O'Connor is being discharged this morning and I wondered what you want me to do.'

'Bring him here before he goes home. I need to have a word with him first.' He hung up as he saw Marsh arrive. 'Good news, Marsh. Father O'Connor is coming out of hospital this morning.'

'I'm glad his injuries weren't too serious,' said Marsh. 'He was lucky to survive that attack.'

'Yes, that blow on the head could have been fatal to a man of his age. I've asked Warner to bring him here before he takes him home.'

'But why are you having him brought here first?'

'It's better than my being seen over in that area. You never know who might be hanging around his place or the club. At least we can talk privately here. It will be nice to see him

143

now that he's got over his head injuries. I know he missed going to the club and seeing the boys. How did your dinner arrangements turn out?'

Marsh gave a broad smile. 'Sally sorted the domestic out and was home within an hour or so.'

'No arrest needed?'

'No. She gave them a warning and left them making up.'

'If only all the domestic quarrels were like that. What about a coffee?'

'Don't you want to wait and have one with the Father?'

'We can have another one when he gets here, Marsh.'

'Some people die from an overdose of drugs. But you'll probably die from coffee poisoning caused by an overdose of caffeine.'

'I thought you liked coffee too.'

'And that's your fault. I could have you arrested for being a coffee pusher and getting people hooked.' Marsh walked to the door and casually asked, 'Large or small?'

'Small.' Bill grinned and added, 'But I'll have a large one when Father O'Connor gets here.'

★　★　★

The hair on Bob Plummer's face had now grown a sufficient length. With careful use of the scissors, he produced a neat goatee beard and moustache and he was able to clean the remainder of his face with a safety razor. So far, he had been pleased with the result of his efforts, but now he had to dye his new creations to match the auburn colour of the hair on his head. After various considerations he decided it would be a lot easier to apply the dye with a toothbrush. It was over an hour later that he stood in front of the mirror admiring his new appearance. He had passed the time the previous day cutting out various letters from a newspaper and sticking them on notepaper to make words. He had used plastic gloves from a garage to avoid leaving any fingerprints and posted it. Today he wanted to call Pat but he knew she wouldn't be in her hotel until after lunch. Patience was not one of his virtues, so he decided he would go for a walk as he was no longer afraid to be seen by anyone. He checked the piece of paper with dates and names of the hotels that she would be staying in. Today she was due at the Hillman Hotel on Tottenham Court Road. He walked to the nearest branch of his bank and checked his account at the hole in the wall. He stood looking at the figure of £261. He only had forty left from the hundred he'd received from Joe Levin, so he knew he would need to be careful until more money came his way. He took out just £50 then caught a bus to Oxford Street. He knew he could pass the time looking round the shops there until it was time to call Pat. Tonight he intended to ravish her body and make up for the few days he had been without any sex.

He was in John Lewis when he caught sight of a man he had become friends with in prison. Steve Saunders was a professional pickpocket and had been released after serving a six-month sentence. Plummer had often wondered where Steve was, and he was pleased to see him again. Suddenly the two men were facing each other and as Steve went to move out of the way, Bob Plummer spoke.

'Steve. It's me, Bob.'

The frown on Steve's face became a smile. 'The voice I'd know anywhere but what happened to the face!'

'I felt like a change. Have you got time to have a drink?'

Steve checked his watch. 'I'm meeting my wife at the car park but I've got another half an hour to pass yet. I could have a coffee with you and you can tell me what you're doing now that you're out.'

They followed the sign to the coffee shop, where Plummer ordered and paid for two coffees. They sat at an empty table and while Steve poured the contents of the sugar bag into his cup, he repeated his question. 'So what *are* you doing, Bob?'

'Trying to find a way to make money, Steve, that's what I'm doing. I've got a new woman in my life now and she thinks I'm working as a private eye.'

Steve laughed. 'I can imagine you doing many things but that isn't one of them. Is that why you've changed the way you look?'

'Well, it works, doesn't it? You didn't recognize me.'

'That's true. So what kind of job are you looking for?'

'I don't care what it is as long as it gives me money.'

Steve was thoughtful as he sipped his coffee. 'How would you like to work with *me* for a while?'

'Doing what?'

'It's an idea that I've thought about but I would need an assistant to make it work.'

'So tell me about it,' said Plummer eagerly.

Steve lowered his voice, making sure nobody else could hear what he was about to say. 'You've got a new lady and want her to think you've got a job, but you need money to impress her, right?'

'Right.'

'Well, I've got a wife I need to keep happy. So you and me both need money but we don't fancy nine-to-five jobs. So my idea would be perfect to make us a lot of money.'

Two women came to the next table and Steve knew it was dangerous to continue the conversation. 'Let's go to the car park. I can explain everything in the privacy of the car.' Both men finished their coffee and Steve led the way. The car park was just outside the rear entrance of the store and they were soon sitting in Steve's Jaguar saloon. 'I'll be quick in case my wife is early, for a change. Now listen, my idea is this: we go to a bank machine and you get behind a person and watch them punch in their pin code. People are warned to cover their number but most don't. Write down their number and give me the nod. Once they have the money and move away from the machine. I'll accidentally bump into them while they're opening their purse or wallet to put their card back. As their things fall out, you come over and help them. In the confusion I shall switch their card for one from the same bank. Then we walk innocently away.'

'Sounds a great idea but where do you get the card to switch from?'

'I kept them from wallets I got at the races. I'm a good dip, Bob,' he said proudly.

'Why do they call pickpockets dips?'

'We dip our hands into someone's pocket,' said Steve, smiling. 'So what about my idea? Are you willing to give it a try?'

'Too right I am.'

'How do I contact you to set it up?'

'I'm not sure where I'll be at the moment. Can I call you?'

Steve wrote down his number on the back of an old carpark ticket. 'If a woman answers, it'll be my wife, Eileen. I'll tell her you're a private investigator that I helped a long time ago and you came to visit me in prison because you are a nice man.' He grinned. 'Give me a call and we can fix a day and give my idea a dry run.'

'I look forward to it, Steve.'

Plummer got out of the car and walked back to pass the time in John Lewis. He was excited at the prospect of having money again and he intended to enjoy his night with Pat even more.

★ ★ ★

Father O'Connor was looking a lot better than Bill Forward thought he would. He got up and greeted him with a smile.

149

'Come in, Father. Have a seat. Would you like a coffee?'

Father O'Connor sat and said, 'That would be nice, if it isn't too much trouble.'

'No trouble at all. I was just going to have one myself.'

Marsh gave him a quick glance of disapproval, then said, 'Milk and sugar, Father?'

'Milk, but no sugar.'

Marsh phoned the canteen and ordered the coffees.

'How are you feeling?' asked Bill.

'Happy to be out of the hospital. Mind you, they did look after me. But I shall be glad to sleep in my own bed again.'

'Have you had any further thought on who it was that hit you?'

'I saw nothing except the shoes, nothing at all — apart from the pavement, of course. But I think I *heard* something. It came back to me when I was leaving the hospital this morning.'

'What was it?' asked Marsh.

'A lady was helping a patient into her car and her bracelet made a sound. It was the sound I think I heard that day.'

'What sort of sound?' asked Bill.

'A sort of chink-chink sound, like you hear with a lady's bracelet.'

Bill and Marsh gave each other a look.

'Or a bracelet that's being worn by a man.

We mustn't forget that men wear jewellery these days, Father,' said Marsh.

'I know one or two of the boys wear gold chains round their necks, but I don't think I know a man who wears what I would call jewellery.'

'We do. And he wears grey shoes with brass pieces,' said Bill.

'And he deals in drugs,' said Marsh. 'I think we should call on our friend Mike Long and get him to talk to us again.'

Bill nodded in agreement. 'Yes. And with a bit of luck, we can convince him that we now have film from a CCTV camera showing the man that struck you, Father.'

The coffees arrived and Marsh handed them round.

'Now remember this is your first day out of hospital, so take it easy. There's no need to rush. When you've finished your coffee I'll get the unmarked car to take you home.'

The priest looked confused. 'I thought the CCTV camera in Conway Street had been put out of action by vandals. Are you saying it's now working again?'

'I know it's a sin to tell a lie, Father, but yes, that's what I'll be saying,' said Bill. 'And to be honest, if I thought it would bring a criminal to justice, I would even lie to your Pope.'

A smile came over the priest's face as he said, 'And in your case he would probably forgive you.'

Within a few minutes, Father O'Connor was on his way home and Bill and Marsh were heading for the home of Michael Kenneth Long. They were followed by PC Roberts, which irritated Bill. When they arrived outside the house, Roberts parked and Bill noticed someone look out from an upstairs room.

'I think that was Long, looking out to see who's turning up. If it was him I bet his wife will say he's not at home at the moment.'

'Let's go and find out,' said Marsh.

Roberts watched them get out of their car and walk up to the front door. As they rang the doorbell, Bill looked back and casually gave Roberts the thumbs-up sign. Mike Long's wife answered the door and looked surprised to see them.

'Oh, hello, aren't you the gentlemen who called before?'

'Yes, we are,' said Bill. 'Could we have a quick word with Mike, please?'

'I'm afraid he's not in at the moment. I don't know if he is coming back today or not,' she said.

Bill gave an enquiring look and said, 'Oh, I thought I saw a man looking out of the

152

upstairs window when we arrived.'

She reacted quickly and said, 'Oh, that would have been the decorator. We're having the room done up. Can I give Michael a message?'

'Yes. Tell him not to get the paint on his lovely clothes. I'll be in touch with him.'

Bill and Marsh went back to their car and drove away as she closed the door.

Marsh chuckled. 'Her face was a picture when you said, 'Tell him not to get the paint on his lovely clothes.' What do you think he'll do now?'

'He'll wonder what we wanted and start sweating, which will ruin his lovely, expensive shirt,' said Bill with a grin.

★ ★ ★

Pat Harrison arrived earlier than usual at her hotel and went to her room to do her paperwork. She arranged with the reception-ist to have lunch in the sandwich bar then began to work on her laptop. She had not had to see many clients and was able to get through her work very quickly. It was just a few minutes before noon that she went to get a sandwich. As she got in the queue, she went to turn her mobile off but changed her mind and left it on in case Bob called. She took her tray along the row and collected a cup of coffee. She paid the cashier then went to an empty table for two and sat down. As she tucked into her sandwich, she was unaware of the well-dressed young man that had taken an interest in her. She was thinking of Bob and hoping she would soon experience another night of carefree sex with him. She was allowing her imagination to run wild when she suddenly noticed the man who was looking at her. He was very good-looking, in his thirties. Her libido had been stimulated by her thoughts of Bob, and she now felt even more excited as her new admirer gave her a warm smile. Pat was tempted to smile in return but, knowing that Bob could arrive early, decided not to. The last thing she wanted was for him to see her involved with another man and cause a scene. She finished her sandwich and coffee and got up to leave. It was as she got to the door she was aware of her new admirer at her side. He opened the door for her and stood back, smiling. He was incredibly young and handsome. She returned his smile and said in her soft, warm voice, 'Thank you.'

'You're welcome. I think a gentleman should always open a door for a lady.'

'I'm afraid there aren't many gentlemen about these days. But I suppose there aren't many ladies either.'

They were walking towards the bar before Pat realized it. She was quite happy to listen to him talk with what she felt was the voice of a well-bred, educated man.

'Some of the younger women today will simply walk past without even a thank you,' he said. 'Will you join me for a drink?'

'That would be nice but first I have to make a phone call. It won't take long.'

'Good. I'll go and get them lined up. What will you have?'

'I'd like a gin and tonic with ice and lemon, please.'

He went into the bar and she walked out of his hearing and spoke to the receptionist. 'There hasn't been anyone asking for me, has there?'

'No, miss.'

'Well, if a Mr Wilson phones, tell him I am at a meeting and will be back in an hour or so.'

'All right, miss.'

'If he should arrive and I am still in the bar, would you ask him to wait in the lounge, please, and then come and warn me? The two gentlemen are business rivals and I don't want them knowing that I'm talking to both of them, you understand.'

'Yes, of course, miss.'

'Thank you.' Pat returned to the bar, hoping Bob would not arrive until she knew more about her young admirer. He was the man that interested her at the moment and she went over to join him at the bar.

'There's a table round the corner if you would like to sit,' he said.

The table was just out of sight from the entrance and she was happy to sit there, knowing that Bob wouldn't be able to see her if he passed the door. Her admirer took her gin and tonic and his vodka and lime and, as she sat, placed them on the table. He introduced himself. 'I'm John, by the way.'

'Hello, John. I'm Pat.' She smiled and raised her glass to him. 'Cheers.'

'Cheers.' He touched her glass with his and they drank. 'So what brings you to this hotel, Pat?' he asked. 'Business or pleasure?'

'Business. I work for a firm of solicitors. I look up people that have been left something in a will and inform them of their good fortune.'

'Sounds interesting. I hope they show their gratitude for your efforts by giving you something.'

'No, I'm afraid people working for legal firms rarely get gifts.' She smiled. 'What about you, what do you do?'

'I'm a financial adviser with an investment

company in Singapore. I travel the world advising people of sound investments that can make rich men richer.'

Pat was surprised. 'But surely you haven't come to this hotel to meet a rich man?'

He gave a chuckle. 'No, Pat. I would normally meet them at one in Park Lane. But I'm not here to meet anyone in my professional capacity. I came to meet a man I haven't seen for years, and as he lives round the corner from here he suggested this place.'

'Oh, I see. Do you live in Singapore?'

'I do when I am not travelling.'

'So your family are out there. I assume you are married?'

'No wife or family for me to worry about, Pat. I live in a nice apartment out there but it isn't big enough to have children running about in. No, the only family I have are my parents and they live just outside the city. My father went out there on business shortly after the war. He met my mother and stayed there. But what about you, are you married? Say no and I'll get us another drink.' He raised an eyebrow as he waited for her reply.

She held her empty glass out and said, 'No.'

He took both glasses and went back to the bar. Pat watched him walk out of sight, wishing she knew how much time she had before Bob arrived. She had no doubts about

John's intention to get her into bed and this excited her. She was letting her imagination run away with her when he returned with their drinks.

'The bar's getting busy,' he said.

'I thought it would,' said Pat.

'I'm afraid someone will come and join us at this table, so why don't we go to my room or yours? At least we will have privacy and be able to talk.'

'Let's make it your room. I might get called to meet a man and tell him that he is the recipient of a rather nice legacy in a relative's will.'

'What a lucky man.'

'I must leave a message at the desk. What is your room number?' asked Pat.

'It's suite five on the first floor.'

'I'll only be a moment.' She went to the girl at reception. 'I am expecting a Mr Wilson at some time. Would you explain that I am at a meeting and ask if he would please wait for me in the lounge? You remember, I spoke to you earlier.'

'Yes, miss. I know what to say.'

'Thank you,' said Pat. She walked up to the first floor, wondering what suite five would be like as she knocked. John opened the door on to a comfortably furnished sitting room with two sofas and armchairs with a coffee table between. There was a folding table and two chairs that made a private dining area. A large flat television screen was attached to the wall. John had put their drinks on the coffee table and as Pat sat on the sofa she could see the open door looking into the bedroom, with its large double bed very prominent. John sat on the sofa next to her and passed the gin and tonic to her.

'We don't have to rush. We have ages before my friend gets here,' he told her. 'Cheers.' As he drank he ran his tongue over his lips in a provocative way that she found sexy. What with that and the open bedroom door, Pat wondered how long he would take before trying to get her into his bed. She didn't have long to wait before he made the next move.

'Let me show you the other room. You can tell me what you think of the décor.' John stood and offered his hand to her but, not wanting to appear eager, she remained seated.

'If it's anything like this room I can tell you exactly what I think of the décor. The word awful springs to mind.'

John offered his hand again and said quietly, 'Come and see if you still think that when you see it from the inside.'

She put her drink down and went to the bedroom with him. Her heart began racing as he closed the door behind them.

12

After a quick lunch in the canteen, Bill Forward went back to his office to find Marsh talking on the phone.

'Yes, I'll tell him. Goodbye, Father.' He hung up. 'That was Father O'Connor to say he got home safely and thank you for keeping an eye on him while he was in hospital.'

'I suppose he will be down at the club now. He really does miss it when he's not there,' said Bill.

'What's his home like?'

'He lives in an old house which has been made into two flats. He has the ground floor and a retired couple have the upstairs. They have their own entrance so they are quite secluded when they want to be. The man looks after the garden and does any odd jobs and she makes the Father his meals and does the cleaning. It all works very well.'

'He seems to be liked by everyone.'

'He is by the people that really know him. But he's had a lot of unpleasant things said about him.'

'Like what?'

'Like when he first opened the boys' club.

Some vicious tongues started rumours that he was homosexual and only interested in the boys for their bodies. As you can imagine, he was terribly upset by that.'

'So what did he do?'

'There are some rough diamonds among those boys and their fathers went around threatening anyone they heard were spreading the rumour. It soon calmed down and most people trusted their priest anyway, but it was nasty at the time.'

'I couldn't imagine the old chap hurting any of his boys.'

'Of course he wouldn't.'

Marsh picked up a letter and took it to Bill. 'This came for you with the midday post.'

Bill looked at the envelope, which showed that the letter was posted in London the previous day. The name and address had been written in capital letters. When he opened the envelope he saw letters that had been cut from a newspaper and stuck on notepaper to make a message. 'Would you believe it! This is from Plummer.'

'You're kidding!'

'No, Marsh, I am not kidding.' He took a plastic bag from a cupboard and dropped the envelope and notepaper into it.

'What does it say?' asked Marsh anxiously.

'It says, 'I'll be in touch, Sergeant.' Better

get this over to the lab. I want it checked for fingerprints. You never know, he might have been careless.' Bill carefully sealed the plastic bag and handed it to Marsh. 'And as he had to lick the envelope, get them to do a DNA as well.'

Marsh took it and looked through the plastic bag at the address. 'The name on the envelope is 'Detective Inspector'. So his reference to you as 'Sergeant' tells you straightaway who it's from. I won't be long.'

As Marsh left the office, Bill thought about Plummer and wondered where in London he was. For once he was glad to be under twenty-four-hour surveillance by Roberts and Walker and happy that Jane had Ruth with her when he was away from home. He wondered what Plummer was looking like now and wished he wasn't so damned clever at avoiding detection. He rang Superintendent Lamb and told him about the letter.

'If Plummer is sending you mail I want anything that is addressed to you intercepted and checked. Just in case he sends you something lethal, do you understand?'

'Yes, sir.'

'And the same thing applies to anything sent to your home. Tell your wife to open nothing until it has been given the all-clear. We never know what this lunatic might do.'

'I'll call her straightaway, sir. And I'll explain the position to the WPC that's with her.'

'Do that. I'll have a word with our fingerprint lads and tell them to make it priority. Don't worry, Forward, we shall have this bloody man back inside eventually.'

'I certainly hope so, sir.' As soon as he hung up, Bill rang Jane. 'Hello, love. Have you had any mail delivered there today?'

'There was only a letter from Dave and Carol. Why?'

Bill was relieved. 'It's just that Bob Plummer sent a letter to me here at the station and there is a possibility, and it is just a possibility, that he might send something nasty to the house.'

'What do you mean by nasty?' Jane asked.

'Who knows what a sick mind might conjure up? The thing is, we don't want you opening anything. OK?'

Jane wasn't sure what was going on but agreed. 'Yes. But I don't think Dave or Carol would send us anything nasty.'

'No, of course not, but I don't want you opening anything in a large brown envelope. Put Ruth Cunningham on.'

Jane passed the phone to Ruth and Bill gave her the same instructions but put more emphasis on the possible danger involved.

Ruth knew that the possible danger he referred to could be serious. She had seen the result on a victim's face from an acid package sent through the mail. But her expression gave nothing to make Jane feel too concerned. 'Yes, sir. I understand,' Ruth said casually.

Bill put the phone down and wondered what Plummer would do next. After a few minutes, Marsh returned from the laboratory.

'They will let us know the results as soon as they've given the letter and envelope a thorough check.'

'So now we wait. But that doesn't mean we do nothing. See if WPC Barbara French is in, and if she is I'd like to see her.'

'Right.' Marsh rang the duty room and found that she was on duty. He got through to her and asked her to come to the office. Within a few minutes, she was facing the inspector.

'Thanks for coming, French. I want you to be the lady from the Inland Revenue again and make another appointment to see Mike Long. Tell him you just want to check the make of his suits or whatever. I don't mind what excuse you give him. As soon as you have an appointment, Marsh and I will visit him with you. He'll open the door for you whereas if we go on our own his wife will say he's out on business. And I need to see him personally. I want to watch his face when I tell him we've got a CCTV image of the man that attacked an elderly priest.'

'When would you like me to call him, sir?' she asked.

Bill looked at his watch. 'See if you can make a date to go and see him later this afternoon. If not, tomorrow morning.'

'I'll go and do that now, sir,' she said and left.

Bill clenched his fist and said, 'It would be nice to nail that bugger.'

'I know. Well, I don't think there can be any doubt that it was him who knocked Father O'Connor to the ground. And with him wearing that bracelet, I reckon we've got him by the short and curlies.'

'I hope you're right and I wish that's where I had Bob Plummer,' Bill sighed. 'Either he's in hiding or he's changed his appearance to the point where he can just wander about without any fear of being recognized.'

'There's one thing we're overlooking, of course.'

'What's that, Marsh?'

'He may not be anywhere near London. He might have got someone to post that letter for him. It might have been someone coming here by bus or train.'

Bill said patronizingly, with a smile, 'I

wondered when you would see that possibility, Marsh.'

Marsh gave him a look of disbelief. 'You had already thought of that, I suppose.'

'No, to be perfectly honest, but as an inspector I shouldn't have to worry about those things. I've got a sergeant to do that for me. A sergeant whose superior I'm proud to be. And there's something you can do that would make me a lot prouder.'

Marsh sighed as he said, 'I know. Get you a coffee.'

Bill looked shocked and said, 'I must have the only young sergeant who is not only a policeman but a mindreader!'

Marsh shook his head and gave a mock contemptuous look as he left the office. Bill walked to the window and looked out. He thought about the strange letter from Plummer and had a feeling he was out there somewhere, planning his next move. He wished someone had seen him and wondered what was going on in his warped mind. After a few moments his thoughts were interrupted when WPC French knocked and entered.

'I have spoken to Mr Long and arranged to see him at 2.45 this afternoon, sir.'

'Thank you, French, Sergeant Marsh and I will arrive as soon as we see you go into the house.' He looked at his watch. 'Meet us here half an hour before and you can lead the way.'

'Right, sir.'

'Marsh and I will keep a discreet distance behind you.'

As she left the office, Marsh arrived with two coffees. 'The one on the left is yours. It's got more sugar than mine.'

Bill looked at the two mugs and hesitated. 'Is that the one on your left or my left?'

Marsh pushed the mug in his left hand towards Bill and asked, 'How did she get on with Long?'

'She's seeing him at the house at 2.45.'

'Great. And us?'

'We will call on him as soon as she is inside and be a nice surprise for him. And this time he won't have to pretend he's the decorator.' Bill smiled. 'I can't wait to see his face when I tell him we've got that CCTV image.'

'There's one thing we haven't accounted for,' said Marsh.

'What's that?'

'What if he refuses to talk unless his solicitor is present? He's one man that is sure to ask if he can see the CCTV film. You know what that John Hall is like.'

'You're right, Marsh. But I'm banking on my idea working and if I'm right he will walk into the trap before he has the chance to call his legal brain.'

Marsh was interested to see how his inspector was going to approach Mike Long and was looking forward to the next meeting between them.

★ ★ ★

Pat Harrison was back in her own room and disappointed at her experience with John. He was younger and much more handsome than Bob but nowhere near as exciting in bed. This good-looking man had not been the lover she had imagined and although he may have satisfied a woman of less experience in the art of lovemaking, Pat was a woman of the world. She had known men twice his age, able to make passionate love with her more than once. Now she would prepare herself for Bob, the perfect bed companion but still a mystery to her. She wondered how dangerous his work as a private detective really was and what kind of income he received. And she wondered if he had changed his appearance much and if so, what would he look like? Her telephone rang and she quickly answered it. 'Hello?'

'Hello, Miss Harrison. I believe you were expecting my call.'

Bob's voice was unmistakable and she was pleased to hear him. 'I am expecting a Mr

Wilson to call. Would that be you, sir?'

'As long as I can see you, I'll be anyone you like,' he said.

'I've missed you, Bob. These last few days have seemed a bit odd without seeing you.'

'I know the feeling,' he said in a quiet, sexy voice. 'I hope you haven't succumbed to another man in my absence.'

'You're enough man for me. But what about all those young, sex-starved girls you've been copulating with? You must be exhausted.'

'Invite me to your room and I'll show you.'

She was already feeling sexy as she asked, 'Where are you?'

He whispered jokingly, 'Having sex with the receptionist. What is your room number?'

She smiled to herself. 'Are you really downstairs?'

'No, but I'm just round the corner. I can be there in a few minutes.'

'Room seven, first floor.'

'I'm on my way and I hope you recognize me.' He rang off.

She checked herself in the mirror again and wondered if the rest of the day would be as sexually exciting as she imagined it would be. Within a few minutes, Bob was at her door. When she opened it she was amazed at the total transformation that was standing in front of her. Not one of Bob's friends would

169

instantly recognize him now. He stood smiling at her obvious surprise in his appearance.

'Well, aren't you going to invite me in?' he said.

'Sorry, Bob, come in. It's just that I can't believe the way you have changed. It's incredible.'

He walked into the room and as she closed the door he took her in his arms. 'Come here and give an old stranger a kiss.'

Pat responded by doing just that and for a moment they were locked in a passionate embrace. The neat beard and moustache seemed to feel sexier and was no comparison to the kisses John had given her. After a while, Bob took his coat off and sat down.

'Well, what do you think of the new Bob Wilson?' he asked with a proud smile. 'The colour and style are all my own work.'

'You look great, Bob. You really do. In fact, I think I prefer you to the old Bob. Congratulations.'

'Thanks. Like I told you, I have to change my appearance now and then in my work as a private investigator. I'm glad you like the new me.'

'Oh, I do, very much.' She put her hand on his thigh and stroked it gently as she said, 'And I hope this one can stay around for a while.'

'If you keep doing that I may have to move in with you on a regular basis. What's the bed like?'

'Why don't we try it?' she whispered.

They slowly removed each other's clothes and got into bed.

★ ★ ★

WPC French pulled up just in front of Mike Long's house, went up to the door and rang the bell. Mike looked quite calm and composed as he ushered her in. As he closed the door, Bill and Marsh parked behind French's car and, without wasting any time, also rang the doorbell. WPC French watched Long turn and open the front door again. His face showed surprise as he saw his unexpected visitors.

Bill smiled as he said, 'Sorry, we didn't let you know that we were coming, Mr Long, but we hoped you would be in.'

'Is it important?' asked Long.

'We think so. May we come in, please?'

Long tried not to show any sign of nerves. 'Could you come back later? I've got an appointment with this lady from the Inland Revenue.'

Seeing an opportunity to leave, French walked back to the door and said, 'Oh, that's quite all right, sir. I'll come and see you another day.' As she walked back to her car, Bill and Marsh moved into the hall. Mike Long was nonplussed as Bill looked him in the face.

'You remember me enquiring about your movements on the day the elderly priest was attacked, don't you?'

Long tried to appear calm. 'Oh yes. Someone had shoes like mine, I believe you said.'

'No sir, *you* said that. And the local people thought that the CCTV cameras were not working. But one of them was, and guess what it produced?'

His lips were dry as he replied, 'I've no idea.'

'It's a photograph, a clear image of the man that hit Father O'Connor. It's a man who was wearing shoes identical to yours. It's a man wearing a bracelet identical to yours. In fact, it's a man who is identical to you, Mr Long. Because unless you have a twin brother, it's a photograph of you, isn't it?'

Long was shaking nervously as he said, 'Oh God, I didn't know he was a priest. From the back he looked like a man who owes me money.'

Bill put a hand on Long's shoulder and said, 'Michael Kenneth Long, I am arresting

172

you on suspicion of being involved in the attack made on Father O'Connor, in Conway Street. You do not have to say anything, but it may harm your defence if you do not mention, when cautioned, something which you may later rely on in court. Anything you say may be given in evidence.'

A nervous Mike Long asked, 'What happens now?'

'You will be taken from here to the police station where you will sign a statement admitting your involvement in the attack on Father O'Connor.'

'Can I see my wife and tell her what's happening?'

'Only if Sergeant Marsh or myself are present.'

Long walked to the door leading to the living room and looked in. His wife was standing by the window, looking concerned.

'Ring John Hall and tell him I've got to go to the police station and sign a statement so I need him to be there. Tell him the charge against me is one of assaulting a priest,' Long told her.

His wife was shocked. 'That's ridiculous.'

'Just ring and tell him. I'll see you later.'

Bill took him gently by the arm and they left the house, leaving his wife to call the solicitor.

13

Mike Long had confessed that he attacked the old priest and had signed a written statement to that effect as soon as he was at the police station. He was nervous as he sat in an interview room waiting for John Hall, his solicitor, to arrive. Bill and Marsh stayed with him and wondered how the legal mind would react when he knew that his client had made the written confession. They didn't have long to wait before Hall arrived and started earning his fee. He could see that Mike Long was looking anxious.

'May I ask why my client is being held here?' he asked.

'Your client has been arrested on the charge of making an attack on an elderly priest, Mr Hall,' Bill said, adding, 'And we have his written statement admitting the offence.'

John Hall had the wind knocked out of his sails when he heard that. 'I wish to speak to my client in private, if I may.'

'Yes, of course.' Bill got up from his chair and Marsh followed him out of the room.

John Hall sat opposite his client and said,

'What the hell is all this about you giving them a written confession! Are you mad?'

'I couldn't deny it because they have video from a CCTV of me hitting the old man. I thought that camera had been broken for ages, but now I'm in the shit.'

John Hall was thoughtful and said, 'Well, you've seen the video so we can't argue with them.'

'I haven't actually seen it.'

Hall threw his arms up in desperation. 'Well, if you have not seen it, how do you know it exists?'

'The inspector even described my shoes and bracelet. So he must have seen it,' said Mike Long.

'I wonder,' Hall said thoughtfully. 'I don't trust that man. He's a copper and up to all the old tricks. I think I'll ask to see that video and see what he comes up with.'

Mike Long was confused and asked, 'What do you mean?'

'There could be a chance that you were conned into that written confession, that's what I mean. If only you had waited for me before you put anything in writing.'

'But why would that inspector tell me that he had seen the video if he hadn't?' Long asked.

'He wanted you to admit that you hit the

priest, and that is exactly what you did. Now I've got to think of a way I can provide you with a logical reason for confessing, even though you are completely innocent of that crime.'

'I don't understand,' said a confused Mike Long.

'When he comes back, let me do the talking. And if you are asked, you simply agree with what I say, all right?'

Mike Long nodded. 'OK.'

The door opened and Bill Forward and Marsh looked in. 'Your client has explained what happened?' Bill asked.

'Yes. He claims that you told him you have a CCTV video of his supposed attack on a priest. Is that correct?'

Bill knew what Hall was going to ask and was ready with his reply. 'I think what I said was that one of the cameras seemed to be working, but when we checked we found that was not the case. None of the cameras in Conway Street are in working order at the moment.'

Mike Long had a look of disbelief on his face but Hall raised a hand to stop him from saying anything. 'My client has been in a state of confusion recently, due to business worries. And so he was naturally confused when you told him that you had a video of him attacking the priest. He thought you had seen the attack and that he was responsible. Apparently you told him he was easily identified by his bracelet as well as his shoes.'

'Oh yes. Father O'Connor has a clear image of the man's shoes and his bracelet, both of which are the property of your client,' Bill told him.

Mike Long began to squirm.

'And remember why he said he struck the Father, sir,' said Marsh.

'Oh yes. He said he hit the priest because he looked like a man that owed him money.'

John Hall was not happy and requested that Mike Long be released on bail. He was taken to the custody suite, and because he was charged with causing grievous bodily harm, was held in custody to appear the following morning at the magistrates court. Spending the night in a police cell was the last thing Mike Long had anticipated and as he was taken away he looked frightened.

★   ★   ★

Bob Plummer was lying on the bed with Pat. They were both exhausted after their erotic session together. Pat was almost asleep when her mobile rang. It was her office, to ask if she could change an appointment to meet a client

177

that afternoon instead of the following morning. Pat reached into her bag and opened her diary.

'My first appointment is at 9.30 with Martin Dale. Is that the one you mean?'

'Yes,' said the secretary.

'Well, as I shall be in this area tomorrow I can manage it with no problem. Any time this afternoon will be fine, so will you call Mr Dale or do you want me to?'

'You can ring him and arrange a convenient time, Pat.'

'OK, I'll do that now.' She rang off and gave a sigh. 'I was looking forward to lying here for a while, Bob. But I've got to meet a client, sorry. The good thing is, I won't have to get up so early in the morning.' She leaned over and gave him a kiss.

'What do you want me to do while you're gone?' Bob asked.

'You can stay here and watch television if you want to. I don't mind. Let me phone this Mr Dale and then I'll have a quick shower.'

Pat phoned her client and Bob watched her walk into the shower. She had arranged to meet the client in an hour and he wondered if she would be taking her laptop with her. If not, it would be the chance he had been waiting for. He was wishing he had a mobile phone and knew that Steve Saunders' idea would get him the money he needed. He decided to wait for Pat to leave and use the laptop if it was available. Then he would go out, call Steve and arrange a day for them to try the idea with a real cash dispenser.

Pat came back from the shower and dressed. She took a folder from her briefcase. 'How do I look?'

'Look great and smell even better.' He smiled.

'You're staying here, I take it?' she said.

'I think so. How long will you be?'

'I should be back within two hours.'

'I'll try and last that long. If not, I shall get that young receptionist up to take care of me.'

'You do and I may be forced to damage your wedding tackle,' she joked, then blew him a sensuous kiss and left. Bob went to the shower and when he had finished was pleased to see that her laptop was still there. He dressed and sat at the coffee table. He opened the laptop and was thinking of the one he used at home before his wife went off with his things and divorced him. At least he would get his revenge on the man he blamed for putting him in prison. Using the laptop, he found what he wanted. He now knew how to ruin Detective Inspector Forward's life for ever and make him suffer for what he did to Bob Plummer. All he had to do now was arrange a time and place to meet Steve Saunders, and hope that making money was as easy as Steve had said it would be.

As Bob wondered whether to use the bedside phone to call Steve, he realized how much he needed his own mobile. It would give him complete independence. In the meantime, he would offer to pay Pat for the call, hoping she would put it on her firm's bill. He dialled Steve's number and heard his wife answer.

'Hello.'

'Mrs Saunders?'

'Speaking.'

'This is Bob Plummer, an old friend of Steve's. Is he there?'

'I'll give him a shout.' Her raucous voice called, 'Steve, it's Bob Plummer.'

Bob winced and thought his eardrum would burst when she called out. Then he heard Steve's voice on the line.

'Hello, Bob. What can I do for you?'

'It's about your idea. I wondered when you wanted to try it out, Steve.'

'What about in the morning?'

'Great. Not too early, though. I shall be busy tonight and I need to catch up on my beauty sleep.'

'What about 10.30 then? We can have a rehearsal before we catch the lunchtime people pulling out their cash,' said Steve.

'Fine by me. Where shall we meet?' asked Bob.

'There's a machine in Luke Street, right outside the bank next to the china shop.'

'OK, Steve, I shall see you there in the morning at 10.30. I'm looking forward to it.'

'So am I. There's a fortune to be made if we do it right. See you tomorrow.'

Bob dreamed of having money again and maybe starting a new life abroad somewhere. But first he wanted his revenge on the man he had come to London to find. And now, thanks to the information he had got on Pat's laptop, that was exactly what he could do.

★　★　★

Father O'Connor was sitting in his office at the club when Terry Kennedy put his head round the door. 'Sorry to be a nuisance, Father, but I've just seen that Sutherland man hanging about the club again. Mr Forward said to let him know if we saw him again, remember?'

'Yes, I do. I'll call him right away and you can speak to him.' He dialled Bill's number and Marsh answered.

'It's Father O'Connor here, Sergeant. Terry has something to tell you.'

181

Terry took the receiver and said, 'I've just seen Benny Sutherland outside the club. Mr Forward wanted to know if he came here again.'

Marsh quickly told the inspector and Bill picked up his extension. 'I'm on my way, Terry, and if he looks as though he might leave, get talking to him, try and keep him there. But when we arrive, disappear. I don't want you to be involved.' Bill and Marsh grabbed their coats and hurried to the car.

Terry casually walked round the club and as he looked through a window he saw Benny stop one of the boys who was on his way in. The boy was Kevin, a sixteen-year-old who worked part-time for a supermarket. Benny showed him a small plastic sachet. Kevin tried to walk away but Benny was using his charm to get the boy interested. After a few moments, he was listening to Benny singing the praises of the drug he was pushing. Then the boy pulled out his trouser pocket and showed Benny that it was empty. Benny placed a friendly arm round his shoulder and was obviously telling him not to worry about the money. Terry looked at his watch, hoping the inspector wouldn't be long. He didn't relish the idea of going out to keep Benny there.

Just then, Terry saw another boy walking

towards the club. Benny beckoned the boy to him but he clearly didn't want to know about Benny or what he was offering and walked into the club. The boy was Mark Tully.

'The nerve of that man,' said Mark. 'Fancy showing his face round here after what he did to Ronnie Hicks. He wants locking up.'

'I agree,' said Terry.

'Do you fancy a game of snooker?' asked Mark.

'Yes, in a minute. I just want to see what happens out there. I might have to go and keep him occupied for a while but you carry on and set the table up.'

Mark was confused. 'What do you mean, 'Keep him occupied'?'

At that moment, Father O'Connor came out from his office.

'How can that man be doing what he is in broad daylight? It upsets me to see Kevin looking interested in the filth that man is pushing.'

Terry and the Father were watching Benny while Mark finished setting the snooker table up, ready for play.

'Why don't we go and tell that man to shove off or we'll call the police?' said Mark.

'Any minute now the police *will* be here,' Father O'Connor told him.

'So you've called them.'

'Yes, as soon as I saw him hovering out there.'

'But suppose he walks away before they arrive?'

'That's when I have to go out and try and keep him occupied,' said Terry.

They could see Kevin shaking his head and it looked as though he was about to walk away. Terry was ready to leave the club when Benny took a wad of money from his pocket. He was saying something to Kevin about the money but Terry couldn't make out what it was. Kevin stood for a moment, looking at the money, but then left and made for the club. Terry could see Benny looking disappointed and knew that this might be the only chance he had. He went to a side door and hurried out. He walked round the side of the club so that he came out on to the front road to look as though he was making his way towards the club entrance. Benny saw him and smiled.

'Hello, son.'

'Oh, hello,' said Terry. 'Sorry, I was miles away.'

'You looked worried, son. Is everything all right?'

'I'm fed up, that's all. I can't get a decent job round here.'

'What sort of thing are you looking for?'

'I'll take anything that might earn me some money,' said Terry.

'Are you one of the boys from the youth club?'

'Yes.'

Benny took the sachet from his pocket. 'See this?'

'Yes.'

'Do you know what it is?'

'It looks like powder.'

'But it's not just any old powder. This makes people feel terrific. If you had some of this you'd feel terrific and you could make yourself a lot of money as well.'

'What do you mean?' asked Terry, feigning interest.

'You could sell some to your friends. Once they've tried it they will come to you to buy more. People always want more and that's when you make a lot of money for both of us.'

'How do you mean, both of us?'

Benny gave a friendly smile and said, 'You keep *them* supplied and I keep *you* supplied.'

Terry saw Bill and Marsh pull up. When Benny saw Bill he went to quickly slip the sachet into Terry's pocket but was in too much of a hurry and missed the opening of the pocket. Bill saw the sachet fall to the ground and Benny try to kick it into the gutter.

'You've dropped something, Benny. You'd better pick it up or I will have to arrest you for littering a public highway.'

'It's not mine. It belongs to this young man.' Benny went to point at Terry and was surprised that there was no sight of him. Terry had done what he was told and disappeared.

'Oh, I see. So when we pick it up and put it carefully into a plastic bag, our forensic department won't find any of your finger-prints — just those of a young man who appears to be a figment of your imagination.'

Benny became agitated. 'But he was here. You must have seen him.'

Bill looked round and said, 'Well, there's no-one here now and I haven't got time to waste, Mr Sutherland. Would you turn out your pockets, please, unless you would rather do it at the station?'

Reluctantly, Benny emptied his pockets and two more sachets appeared. Marsh held each one carefully by the corner and put them into a separate plastic bag.

'I don't know what they are. They must have been put there by someone,' said Benny.

'I think they're drugs,' Marsh told him. 'What do you think, sir?'

Bill looked closely at the sachets. 'Yes, but the contents of those look different to each

186

other. Don't you think so, Mr Sutherland?'

'I couldn't tell you. I don't know much about drugs.'

Bill gave him an incredulous look. 'I'll tell you what I think. I think one of those is heroin and the other one is cocaine. The same as the one you dropped when we arrived. And that means you have committed a serious offence. Benny Sutherland, I am arresting you on suspicion of being in possession of a class A drug with intent to supply. You do not have to say anything but it may harm your defence if you do not say, when cautioned, something which you may later rely on in court. Anything you say may be given in evidence. Do you understand?'

'I'm not saying anything until I have seen my solicitor.'

Marsh took his arm and moved to the car. 'You can call him from the station,' he said. He and Benny sat in the back while Bill drove them away, obviously pleased to have got something on Benny at last. When they arrived at the police station, Bill sent the sachets to the forensic lab, asking for them to be treated as urgent. He knew that until it was confirmed that the sachets contained class A drugs, he would be unable to hold Benny in custody. When Hall arrived, he heard what Benny had to say and asked that he be released on bail. They were taken to the custody suite where the custody sergeant made his decision.

'Because we are awaiting forensic evidence at this time, you will be released on police bail and report to a police station each day until the forensic report is completed.'

Benny and John Hall left the custody suite together.

14

Mike Long was tired and worried as he sat waiting to be called into court. John Hall sat next to him and was quietly explaining the procedure to him.

'The magistrates hear what you have been charged with by the clerk of the court. Because you have no previous police record, we will request that you have the charge of causing actual bodily harm dealt with here by the magistrate.'

'I don't understand.'

'Well, if this went to a crown court you could get up to five years for ABH.'

Long buried his head in his hands. 'Oh God.'

'Calm down. Listen to me. If the magistrates deal with it here you will get a six-month prison sentence suspended for twelve.'

'You make it sound like it's nothing. Well, I'm scared and I don't mind admitting it.'

'Will you listen to me, Mike. By pleading guilty you will — ' He was interrupted by the clerk calling Long into court. As they entered the courtroom, gone was the suave Mike

Long. Instead he looked like the nervous man that he was. As he looked at the three magistrates sitting on the bench, he wished he had never got into this mess. The clerk of the court said, 'Are you Michael Kenneth Long?'

'Yes,' Long replied in a weak voice.

'The charge against you is that on the fourteenth of this month you struck down one Father Patrick O'Connor, causing actual bodily harm. How do you plead?'

John Hall looked at the bench and said, 'My client pleads guilty to the charge of causing actual bodily harm, your worship. He requests that his case be dealt with by your worships in this court.'

The chairman of the magistrates looked at the crown prosecutor. 'You have the facts of this case?'

'Yes, your worship.'

'Very well, please proceed.'

The crown prosecutor began. 'On the fourteenth of this month, the defendant struck down a Catholic priest, Father Patrick O'Connor. The attack took place in a street adjacent to a boys' club that the Father ran in order to keep boys off the streets and therefore out of trouble. The priest was taken to hospital where he required eight stitches to heal the head wound made by the attack. There are no previous convictions recorded against the defendant.'

As the crown prosecutor sat down, John Hall got to his feet and said, 'My client has been through much mental aggravation recently, in both his business and private lives. This has caused him confusion. When he saw the priest hurrying along in front of him, he was convinced that he was a man who has owed him a large amount of money for a long time but has refused to pay. He hit the man, with intent to stop him, but as soon as he realized his mistake he tried to comfort the man then called for an ambulance. As your worships have heard, my client has no previous convictions and he deeply regrets the harm he caused the priest and is profoundly sorry.'

Mike Long watched the faces of the magistrates for their reaction to John Hall's statement. The chairman leaned in to his colleagues and the three men were nodding to each other, obviously agreeing. Long stood, anxiously waiting for their verdict.

'Michael Kenneth Long, this court finds you guilty of committing actual bodily harm on Father Patrick O'Connor. You are sentenced to six months imprisonment that will be suspended for twelve months.'

Mike Long was surprised and unable to hide his relief at the lenient sentence. He shook John Hall by the hand and gave a nod of gratitude to the bench as he left the court.

★ ★ ★

Bob Plummer was on his way to meet Steve Saunders in Luke Street as arranged. He had stopped on the way and bought the few things that the information on the laptop said he would need to make DI Forward's gift. But although it appeared simple to make, he would have to be in a place where he could carefully assemble it without interruption. He was anxious to complete it and get it in the post in time for the last collection. Bob had looked forward to doing this for a long time. But right now he knew he had to forget his plan for vengeance and concentrate on seeing how good his memory was for pin numbers.

Steve was already in Luke Street and saw Bob making his way towards the china shop. He managed to attract his attention and signalled him to go to a nearby café.

The interior of the café was in need of redecorating but the cups were china and clean. There was a jolly-looking lady serving and just a few customers sitting at the plastic-covered tables. Steve had ordered two coffees and indicated for Bob to sit at a table away from other customers. Bob sat and waited until Steve joined him. He put the sugar in his coffee and the two men spoke quietly.

'Remember what you have to do?' asked Steve.

'Yes. I make a note of the card pin number and when you *accidentally* bump into the person and knock their wallet or purse to the ground, I distract their attention by helping to pick their things up. And that's when you swap their cards.'

'Perfect. I hope you've got a good memory for numbers.'

'Don't worry, I won't let you down.'

'I know you won't, Bob. Now as soon as I have switched their card and we stand up again, I shall move away. Then you must pretend to use the machine otherwise if someone joins the queue behind you they might think it strange.'

'OK.'

'Right, we'll finish our coffee and do it, yes?'

'Yes.' Bob raised his cup. 'Cheers.'

As they left the café, Bob felt an air of excitement. There was nobody at the cash machine and they stood waiting for someone to come and use it. They did not have long to wait before a middle-aged woman pulled up in a smart BMW. As she walked to the cash machine, Bob Plummer moved behind her. He watched her put her card in and tap in the pin number, which was accepted. The card was then returned and she took it, waiting for the money. It was as she took the money and with the card still in her hand that Steve moved quickly towards her. He bumped into her with perfect timing, sending her purse, bank card and the money to the pavement. Bob immediately stooped down with Steve to help her. Bob held the open purse upside-down so that her loose change fell out and while he and the woman collected it, Steve apologized to the woman for bumping into her and she accepted that it was an accident. Steve quickly switched her card with one he had from an identical bank. He then gave her the card, which she put carefully in a compartment in her purse. Within seconds the plan was complete and the woman got in her car and drove away. They waited until she was out of sight, then Steve put her card into the machine and Bob told him the pin number. Steve chose to see a mini-statement and it showed that she had a good amount in the account. She was allowed to withdraw £250 a day but had only withdrawn £50. Without hesitation, Steve got out £200 which he split equally with Bob and they walked away. Ten minutes later they were sitting in the bar of a public house having a glass of lager.

'I couldn't believe it was so easy. It was just like you said it would be,' said a delighted Bob.

'Yes, it was perfect,' said Steve, smiling. 'I've got another four cards on me, so we can do those banks before lunch. We might make another £300 this morning, who knows?'

'That has got to be the easiest hundred I've ever made. I still can't believe it.'

'As long as we're careful, we can wander round London at our leisure and just pick the banks as we go. As long as we aren't greedy, we can make a small fortune. With my skill and your memory for numbers, we are the perfect team.'

★ ★ ★

After they had finished their drinks they went out and had more success, making a total of £300 each. They agreed to meet up again in two days and Bob went back to the pub. He had noticed that the men's toilet there had a urinal but only one cubicle with a door and that was perfect. He could be alone in there with the door locked and that would give him all the time he needed to make up the present and get it in the post. He smiled as he

195

thought of Detective Inspector Forward getting the full impact of the letter bomb that he was able to make thanks to the information he'd got from Pat's laptop.

★   ★   ★

Superintendent Lamb was becoming more frustrated than ever at the lack of any sightings of Bob Plummer, a fact he made clear when he called Bill Forward to his office.

'This man seems to have simply disappeared and I can't believe he hasn't been sighted somewhere.'

'We know he changed his appearance by dying his hair but it's what he's done since that's a mystery,' said Bill.

'I agree,' sighed Lamb. 'You know I asked the lab to make their report urgent on that envelope you received.'

'Yes, sir.'

'Well, they did and I have their report here,' said Lamb as he pushed it towards Bill. 'You will see that he wore gloves, so his prints were not on it. But they matched his DNA where he licked the envelope.'

'So it was definitely Plummer who sent me that '*I'll be in touch, Sergeant*' message,' said Bill.

Lamb nodded. 'Yes, there's no question, it was Plummer.'

'But how do we find him?' asked Bill. 'He's obviously changed his appearance again so it's like looking for the invisible man.'

'He's bound to make a mistake. His luck can't hold out for ever.'

'That's what Sergeant Marsh keeps telling me.'

'And he's right. Now, changing the subject, I hear that Michael Long got six months suspended for twelve.'

'Yes, sir. His solicitor was John Hall, a shrewd man who will represent any crook if they can afford him.'

'We must keep an eye on Mr Long and hope he makes a mistake and we can catch him drug dealing again. These suppliers and dealers need locking up,' said Lamb.

'I agree, sir. Well, if there's nothing else I'll get back to my office.'

'Off you go, then. And let me know straight-away if you hear anything from Plummer.'

Bill gave an affirmative nod. 'I will.' He left and returned to his office, where Marsh was on the phone.

'The inspector has just walked in. Tell him what you just told me.' Marsh turned to Bill. 'It's Sergeant Cavendish in the post reception department.'

Bill picked up his extension. 'Yes, Sergeant?'

'We were asked to look out for any suspicious mail that was addressed to you, sir.'

'Yes, I know. Has something arrived?'

'Not yet, no, but I've had an outside call from a friend of mine, Ray Turner, who's an ex-copper. He works at the town hall in the security department.'

'And?'

'A man asked him if the addresses on the voters list was kept up to date as he didn't want a gift he was sending to get lost. Ray thought there was something odd about the man and asked which name and address he wanted confirmed. Then the man mentioned the name, Forward. Ray remembered you, of course, from his days here. Anyway, he told the man the address was not on the list.'

'Did he describe this man?' asked Bill.

'Yes. He was a big man with a good head of hair, goatee beard and a neat moustache. Ray was convinced they had recently been dyed.'

'What was the colour?'

'A sort of auburn, he said.'

'Thank Ray Turner for me. He may have left the force but he still has an eye for detail, thank goodness. You know what they say, once a copper always a copper. I might need him to confirm the man's identity once we have him in custody.'

'That won't be a problem, sir. We'll keep an eye on your mail here but you had better look out for anything coming to your home address, just in case.'

'I will, Sergeant, and thank you.' Bill hung up. 'It's got to be Plummer that went to the town hall,' he told Marsh. 'So now we know what he looks like we might have more luck in finding him. Get our art boys to doctor another photo of him with the goatee beard, moustache and auburn hair. I'll get on to WPC Ruth Cunningham and tell her to be extra cautious. Then I shall go along and let Lamb know about this latest development. Well, at last things look as though they're moving in our favour.' He picked up the phone to dial home. 'While I'm doing this, you can get on to those solicitors and find out what hotel that Pat Harrison woman has been to in the last couple of days. Then take an up-to-date photo of Plummer and see if the receptionist at her hotel has seen him around lately.' Bill dialled his home number and Jane answered. 'Hello, love, it's me. Everything all right?' he asked.

'Yes, fine.'

'Good. Put Ruth Cunningham on. I need a word with her.'

Jane passed Ruth the receiver. 'It's my husband — he wants to talk to you.'

'Hello, sir.'

'We have an update on Plummer's appearance. Tell my wife he now has a goatee beard, moustache, and his hair is auburn so keep an eye out for anyone of that description who might come anywhere near the house. Call Roberts on his mobile and tell him.'

'I'll do it right away, sir.'

'I'll get a photo of Plummer out to you as soon as our people have done them. And be extremely cautious. This man might try anything.'

'Don't worry, I'll be careful, sir.'

As soon as he'd hung up, Bill went to tell Superintendent Lamb the latest news on Plummer.

Marsh returned to his desk and phoned the solicitors Pat Harrison worked for, to find out where she was staying.

★ ★ ★

Bob Plummer was safely in the pub toilet with the door locked. He knelt down and used the seat cover as a table. He carefully placed the contents of his purchase in position and was surprised how simple and easy it was to follow the instructions to make

200

a letter bomb. In less than thirty minutes it was ready to seal and address. He finally got up and was glad to stretch his legs. Now he had to get it posted and hoped that when it was opened it would be powerful enough to do the job he had intended. He had used a large padded envelope and was convinced he had followed the instructions perfectly. All he wanted now was to learn that his efforts had been successful. He left the pub and made his way to the main post office. As he stood waiting to be served, he became nervous. He wondered if he had connected the wires correctly but he knew it was too late to open the package now. As the woman took it from him and put it on the scale to weigh it, Bob ducked down and pretended to be adjusting his shoe. He heard the voice of the woman call out the charge and, relieved there was no explosion, stood up and paid her. She thanked him, then he took the change and left the post office. He hoped the next time he heard about his letter bomb was from a newspaper, or the TV, reporting injuries to a DI Forward in Chelsea.

★ ★ ★

Bill returned to his office just as the new photographs had been given to Marsh. Bill took one and compared it with a photograph Marsh was holding.

'I see he's made the hair colour more natural on this one.'

'Yes. He said dyed hair on the head is never the same as on a beard or moustache. The natural texture is different on the head apparently. He's done what he thinks it would look like if it's dyed auburn,' said Marsh.

'Well, I would never recognize this face as Plummer,' said Bill. 'Any luck with the solicitor?'

'Yes. Pat Harrison was at the Hillman Hotel last night but they aren't sure if she's staying tonight as well. I'll get over there with this new photo and see if Plummer's been there.'

'I would like to make a suggestion.'

'What's that?'

'Make sure the receptionist doesn't know you're a copper. She might tip them off and we don't want that. Say you are representing the man's wife and then show her the photo of Plummer and watch her reaction. If it is him who has been staying with Miss Harrison, emphasize that the receptionist must not tell them of your visit otherwise she might end up in court as a witness, et cetera. We don't want her telling them that someone is asking about them.'

'Don't worry, I'll be careful. What if Plummer *is* due there tonight?'

'In that case, we'll arrange a surprise for him, sunshine.'

★ ★ ★

Bob Plummer was pleased with his new mobile phone. The assistant got him on to pay-as-you-go and within a very short time he had registered with the company and been given his phone number. The money he earned with Steve Saunders had been a godsend and he was looking forward to a lot more to come. He took a chance on Pat not being busy and rang her mobile number. She answered and he was excited at using his new toy.

'This is Bob. Can you talk?'

'Yes. I'm glad you've called me. I was going to leave a message for you at the Hillman.'

'Oh. What's the message?'

'I'm not staying there tonight. The woman I was due to see there has been taken to hospital. So now the office has arranged for me to meet a man this morning instead of this afternoon.'

'Does that mean I won't see you tonight?'

'No, it does not. I'm not letting you get off performing your duty that easily. I'm staying at the Romany in Forest Hill. I'll tell them

203

I'm expecting a Mr Wilson to call, shall I?'

'Yes. And tell them Mr Wilson can't wait to perform his duty,' he whispered.

'Oh, lovely, and we won't have to get up early either.'

'By the way, I bought myself a new mobile and you're my first call.'

'I'm flattered.'

'The things I do for you.'

'It's the things you're *going* to do that interest me, Bob.'

'You'll have to wait and see, won't you?'

'I must go. I'll see you later at the Romany.'

★ ★ ★

When Marsh arrived at the Hillman Hotel, the reception was busy with people checking out. He waited until it was quiet then showed the receptionist Plummer's photograph. 'Do you recognize this man?' he asked.

Her reply was immediate. 'Oh, that's Mr Wilson but he's not here now.'

'He was staying here last night, was he?'

'Well, he might have been. He's a friend of Miss Harrison's but she checked out early this morning, so he would have gone anyway.'

'Could you get someone to check the room just to make sure?' Marsh asked her.

Two men came down to reception and

handed in their keys. As they left, the girl phoned the chambermaid.

'Check seven and let me know if it's empty, please. I won't keep you a minute, sir.'

'That's all right,' said Marsh.

Another man came and handed his key in and after a few more minutes the reception phone rang and the girl picked it up. 'Thank you, Helen.' She put the phone down. 'The girl checked the room but it's completely empty, sir.'

'Thank you. Did Miss Harrison give a forwarding address, by any chance?' Marsh asked.

The girl looked at the form the visitor had signed when she checked in. 'It just says Belling and Musgrove and a phone number,' she told him.

'Thank you, miss. You have been very helpful.' Surprised at the ease with which he had got the information, he phoned Bill, who told him to return to the office. When Marsh arrived, Bill Forward greeted him with a smile.

'Nice work, sunshine. So now we know exactly what Bob Plummer looks like. While I was waiting for you I got the new photograph out to all stations in the area.'

'What we need to know is where Pat Harrison is staying tonight. Then if Plummer is going to join her, we've got him by the short and curlies,' said Marsh.

'I know. But we mustn't give her any hint that we are on the lookout for Plummer. If that happens we'll never see him again. He's too cunning to walk into a trap.'

'So what do you suggest we do?'

'I suggest we get a woman in here.'

'I don't think your Jane would like that, sir. And my Sally wouldn't be too pleased.' Marsh grinned.

'I mean we get a woman to call Belling and Musgrove and say she's a friend who was going to call and surprise her at the Hillman but she's checked out and the only address she gave them was Belling and Musgrove, and have they any idea where she is? If a man calls they might get suspicious, but if a woman calls it's more believable that she's a friend of Miss Harrison, agreed?'

'Yes, I think you're right.'

'Of course I'm right. That's why I'm an inspector,' said Bill smiling. 'Go and have a look and see who can do this for us. Then bring her back here.'

'By the scruff of the neck or shall I ask her nicely?' Marsh asked with sarcasm as he left the office.

Bill hoped his idea of a woman phoning would work. He was getting fed up with

Plummer keeping one step ahead of him all the time. And now, with the photograph out there in circulation, he was sure Plummer's luck was about to run out.

Marsh came back to the office with Katherine Brett. She was a police sergeant in her mid-twenties, who Bill knew but had never worked with. 'You know Sergeant Brett, sir.'

'Yes, of course. Come and sit down, Sergeant.'

'Thank you, sir,' she said and sat in the chair beside his desk.

'Did Sergeant Marsh explain what we would like you to do for us?'

'You want me to make a phone call, he said.'

'Yes, but not just an ordinary phone call. As you know we are looking for a villain called Bob Plummer. You should have a photograph of him.'

'We have all been given copies of it, yes, sir.'

'Well, that's who we're really after but to find him we need to know where a certain lady is staying tonight. She and Plummer have been spending time together in her hotels, but we don't know where she's staying tonight, and that's where your phone call is needed.'

'We want you to be a girlfriend of hers,'

said Marsh. 'The company she works for is a firm of solicitors and they put her in hotels for the night, so it's got to sound genuine.'

'You tell them you're a friend of Pat Harrison and you want to pay her a surprise visit but have no idea where she is staying tonight. You don't want to phone her because that would spoil the surprise when you show up. If you just imagine you are only in the country on a short visit, I'm sure you will find your own words to convince them. Do you think you can do this?' asked Bill.

'I think so, sir. I'll do my best anyway.'

Bill lifted the handset on his phone. 'I'll just make a call, and then you can use this phone. Hello, this is DI Forward. I don't want any calls put through to this office until I tell you. Thank you.' He passed the telephone to Sergeant Brett with the number of Belling and Musgrove. Bill listened on his extension. She dialled and a man answered.

'Belling and Musgrove.'

'Oh, hello, I wonder if you can help me. I'm a friend of Pat Harrison. I have just arrived in this country and I want to pay her a surprise visit. I know she always stays in hotels when she works for you and wondered if you know where she's staying tonight.'

'I'm sorry but I can't give you that information.'

'Oh please,' she begged. 'I'm only here overnight and I'd hate to leave without saying hello.'

'I can't give you that information because I have no idea where she might be staying. She didn't say. I can give you her mobile number if that's any help.'

'Thank you.'

Bill listened to her being given the number and wrote it down. Then he quickly wrote down something he wanted her to add before hanging up. Police Sergeant Brett nodded and, putting it in her own words, said, 'I would be grateful if you didn't say anything to Pat about my call. There is a chance that I may get back here in a week or so and I don't want my surprise visit spoilt.'

'I shan't say anything, miss.'

'Thank you.' Katherine Brett rang off. 'Was that OK, sir?'

'Perfect,' said Bill, smiling. 'You were a very convincing liar, Sergeant.'

She returned his smile and said, 'I learnt it at the police training school, sir.' She could see that Bill appreciated her sense of humour. 'Will that be all?'

'Yes, thank you, Sergeant.'

She left the office and Marsh was pleased with himself. 'I thought she was very good. I chose the right one there.'

'You certainly did, Marsh. You seem to have a natural gift for choosing a woman. I wonder who you will choose to get me a coffee?'

'If I wasn't here you would have to call the canteen and get them to send one down to you. Shall I show you how to do that, sir?' Marsh asked, tongue in cheek.

'Would you, Marsh? That is kind of you. And write it down for me so that I won't forget.'

Marsh picked up his phone and tapped in a number. 'Two coffees for DI Forward's office, please.'

'Oh, you should have ordered one for yourself, Marsh.'

Before they could continue their banter, Katherine Brett knocked and came back into the office. 'Sorry to bother you, sir, but I just had a thought.'

'What's that, Sergeant?' Bill asked.

'Well, to find out if Pat Harrison is staying at a hotel tonight, why don't I call her on her mobile and say I'm an old friend who would like to see her while I'm here. Tell her the same story I told the man at Belling and Musgrove. Say I won't tell her who I am because I want to be a surprise when she sees me. Do you think that might work?'

Bill gave Marsh an enquiring look. 'What do you think?'

'It might work. It all depends on whether she believes the story of a friend from the past wanting to surprise her. And there is another thing.'

'What's that?' asked Bill.

'Suppose she isn't staying at a hotel tonight. She might be going home or staying with a friend. In either case, she may not be seeing Bob Plummer, so we are back where we started,' said Marsh.

Bill nodded and looked at Katherine Brett. 'He's right, of course. The last thing we want to do is let Plummer know we're on to him. But thank you for your offer, Sergeant.'

'It was just a thought, sir.'

'And a good one but Marsh is right. We cannot afford to push our luck especially now that we know what Plummer looks like,' said Bill.

'And the name he uses when he does stay at a hotel with her,' said Marsh. 'Maybe Sergeant Brett could give Belling and Musgrove a call in the morning and find out if she is staying at a hotel tomorrow night?'

'Let me think about it. You'll be on duty in the morning, won't you?' Bill asked her.

'Yes, sir.'

'All right, Sergeant, I'll talk to you in the morning.' Katherine Brett said goodbye and left the office.

'She's very keen to help, isn't she?' said Marsh.

'Yes, she is, but we mustn't rush into this without being very careful. We could be damned close to catching the elusive Mr Plummer and I don't want to louse it up. We can't afford to lose him now that we're so close. I told Sergeant Brett I would let her know in the morning and that's exactly what I shall do. But not until I've had a chance to sleep on it.'

'It's been really worrying you, this Bob Plummer business, hasn't it?'

'At first I thought we would have him back in custody in a matter of hours but he's out-smarted us and that annoys me.'

'Your wife must be fed up having Ruth Cunningham there all day as well.'

'It was good of Lamb to agree for Cunningham to keep an eye on Jane and the house while I'm at work. It makes me feel a lot better, I can tell you.'

'Well, fingers crossed, one way or another we shall soon have Plummer inside, where he belongs,' said Marsh.

'I hope you're right, sunshine. I really do.'

15

DI Forward had stayed awake for a long time when he went to bed that night, with his brain working overtime. First he was thinking about Bob Plummer. Then his previous case of the abused child came to mind, soon followed by the attack on Father O'Connor by Mike Long. His tossing and turning had prevented Jane from getting to sleep so she made him a drink of hot chocolate and gave him one of her sleeping pills. Finally he fell into a deep sleep.

It was just gone nine o'clock and he was having a quick breakfast when his phone rang.

'Sergeant Cavendish, post department, sir. Sorry to bother you at home but we have received a padded envelope that's addressed to you. Our security people think it's a letter bomb.'

'Christ! What have they done with it?'

'An explosives expert has taken it away to make it safe.'

'I hope he can. We need to know where it was posted and if there are any fingerprints,' said Bill.

'I noted the postmark, sir. It was posted in London and caught the last collection yesterday in WC1. Once it has been made safe, forensics will go over it for any prints.'

'Thank you, Sergeant. I shall be in my office in half an hour.'

Because of traffic congestion it was an hour before Bill arrived at his office and he was surprised to see Marsh looking at a forensic report.

'They haven't got a result on that letter bomb, *surely*?'

'No. This is the tests they did on Benny Sutherland's drug sachets,' said Marsh.

'And?'

'Just as we thought — two cocaine and one heroin.'

'Well, as there's nothing to do here until we know where Plummer is, I think we should go and charge Sutherland for being in possession of, and trying to push, class A drugs on our patch, don't you?'

'I certainly do. It'll be nice to get another one off our streets.'

'Yes, it will. And as soon as Benny is inside we can phone Father O'Connor and young Terry and give them the news. And if we can trace Plummer's whereabouts, this may turn out to be a good day after all,' said Bill, smiling.

★ ★ ★

Pat Harrison opened her eyes and saw Bob trying to find a channel on the television set.

'What are you doing?' she asked him.

'I am trying to see if there's any local news on this TV.'

She sat up and wiped her eyes. 'Why, has something happened?'

'That's what I'm trying to find out.'

She was confused. 'How do you mean?'

'I mean what I said. I'm trying to see if anything *has*! For Christ's sake, be quiet for a minute!' he snapped.

'Don't shout at me like that.'

'Shut your face, for fuck's sake! I'm trying to listen!'

Pat couldn't believe he was speaking to her like that and looked angry. She got out of bed and went to the bathroom. 'When I come back I want you out of here. And I mean *out*. No man speaks to me like that.' She closed the door and locked it.

Bob realized he had come on too strong.

★ ★ ★

Benny Sutherland was picked up and charged with being in possession of class A drugs with intent to supply. He had no record of

215

previous convictions and Bill knew he would only get six months. But for someone like Benny, his first taste of life in a prison would be unbearable. Like Mike Long, Benny would miss his expensive clothes and food at the best restaurants. After he was charged Bill and Marsh went back to their office where there was a message from Sergeant Cavendish at the post department to give him a call. Bill lost no time in ringing his number.

'It's DI Forward. Have you got news for me, Sergeant?'

'Yes, sir. The letter bomb was easily made safe. It seems it was quite a primitive type, made up of simple ingredients. The envelope is intact apart from a slit where it was opened to disconnect the wiring and there were some prints you can check with your suspect's record. Unless he wore gloves they should be there along with the postmen who handled it. I'll send it up to you, sir.'

'Thank you, Sergeant. I owe you a drink.' He hung up.

'Good news?' asked Marsh.

'Yes. Cavendish is sending the envelope up so that we can check the prints on it. We know Plummer sent the thing to me. Let's hope his prints are on it somewhere.'

'I'll get his record file up here,' said Marsh as he left the office.

Bill was feeling better about the case and wondered if this was a good time to get Katherine Brett to call Belling and Musgrove. He decided to let Superintendent Lamb know what was happening first.

★　★　★

Bob Plummer waited until Pat came out of the bathroom. He walked over to her and took her in his arms.

'I'm sorry, Pat. I shouldn't have spoken to you like that. In my job I've got to do some rotten things and one of them is to find a policeman and see if he's been injured. That's why I was listening to local news, to know how he was.'

Responding to his holding her, she liked the feel of their naked bodies touching and her anger subsided. 'It was the way you used the F-word and told me to shut up that hurt,' she said.

He smiled and in a quiet voice said, 'You don't mind me using the F-word when we're making love, though.'

'That's different,' she whispered, as she felt him getting aroused. She wanted him to pull her back on to the bed again and in a matter of moments he had. The two of them found their sexual desires as strong as they ever were and needed time to get their strength back before leaving the hotel.

★ ★ ★

Superintendent Lamb was concerned that Plummer had sent the letter bomb even though he'd a feeling he might try something.

'Well, he's obviously determined to hurt you one way or another. At least he has shown his hand and we must be thankful his effort to make the letter bomb was, as the disposal chap called it, 'primitive'. Otherwise God only knows what damage it might have done.'

'I know. And thank heaven it wasn't sent to my home. He tried to get my address from the list of voters, remember.'

'Well, fortunately police officers' private details are never given on those. But that does give us another problem.'

'What's that, sir?'

'He'll want to know if his bomb has been successful and if you've been injured, so what shall we do about that? If we put a piece in the paper or on local radio or TV saying police officer injured by letter bomb, he might think he's been successful and leave London for good.'

Bill was thoughtful and then he said,

'Suppose, we say the injured police officer is in a certain hospital but don't mention his name. Plummer is sure to turn up to find out what damage was done and if the police officer was me. That might be the one trap he won't be able to avoid falling into. His curiosity will be too strong.'

Lamb gave a nod of approval. 'Fancy a day in hospital, do you?'

'I'll do anything to get Plummer put away.'

'We'll get an ambulance to come and get you. They can bandage your hands to make it look as though they're injured. And put some more bandage round your head to suggest that part of your face was damaged. We have to make it look genuine to anyone watching from outside,' said Lamb. 'Now go to your office and I'll get the ambulance here and get our press office to tell the radio and TV people about the incident.'

Bill hurried back to his office. Marsh was looking at the letter bomb envelope and copies of fingerprints from the Bob Plummer file.

'He must have been in a hurry when he made this. His prints are all over it,' said Marsh.

'Now listen. The super and I have come up with an idea to bring Plummer out of hiding.'

'What's that?'

'I'm going into hospital and the injuries to a senior police officer will be announced on radio and TV without giving my name. That should be enough to get Plummer to check on the identity of the injured police officer. I'll be in bed with injuries to my hands and face.'

'You'll have an armed officer there, I hope.'

'Oh yes, Roberts will be around, don't worry. I'm taking no chances where Plummer is concerned.'

'Suppose he doesn't go to the hospital but gets someone else to check on the condition of the wounded copper?' said Marsh. 'Plummer would be happy to know that his letter bomb had caused damage to your face and hands. But then he might disappear, never to be seen again. What then?'

'That's a good point, Marsh. The only place he might go to in London is a hotel where the Harrison woman is going to be staying. We need to know where she will be tonight.'

'Do you want me to get Sergeant Brett to give her a call?'

'No. You call her,' said Bill.

'Me?'

'Yes. It's always possible that wherever she is, Plummer might be with her. If Brett phoned her it might be too soon after her last call. But if a man called to say that his cousin is arriving in London early this evening and has asked him to arrange a convenient time for her to meet Miss Harrison, that will sound more believable, won't it?'

'Yes, she might buy that.'

'And don't give her any other information such as names. Remember, your cousin wants her visit to be a surprise.'

'When do you want me to call her?'

Bill looked at his watch. 'It's pot luck whether she will answer. If she's with a client she might be on voicemail. In which case say nothing and try again later.'

'OK.'

The door opened and Superintendent Lamb walked in. 'I take it you have explained to Marsh what we're arranging.'

'Yes, sir,' said Bill.

'Good. If anyone sees DI Forward being taken to the ambulance and wants to know what's happened, it was an incident with a letter bomb, and that's all you can say, is that understood, Sergeant?'

'Yes, sir,' said Marsh.

'The ambulance will be here in a minute and they know what to do. Roberts will be at the hospital as a male nurse, and I'll have other firearms people there, so this time I don't think Plummer will escape the long arm of the law.'

'I hope not. He's been free too long as it is,' said Bill.

'What if these ambulancemen let the cat out of the bag?' asked Marsh. 'How do you know you can trust them?'

'I know because they are Metropolitan police officers who are trained for this kind of situation. Usually they attend the officers injured in street riots. Don't worry, they know what they have to do,' said Lamb.

A knock at the door prompted Marsh to open it. Standing there were two ordinary-looking ambulancemen who were quickly ushered in.

'We need to show injuries to the face and hands,' Lamb reminded them.

'How much of the face needs bandaging?' asked one.

'If you can keep it just above the eyes so that I can see if Plummer turns up.'

'Leave it to us,' said the second man, who had bandages at the ready and started work on Bill's head.

'By now, the radio and television people should start putting it out that a senior police officer was injured by a mystery package. The press will have it in their papers this evening starting with their early editions this after-noon,' Lamb told him.

'Well, that's good news. I'd hate to think

that I was going through all this for nothing,' said Bill.

The ambulancemen had him bandaged and ready to go within minutes. He was carried on a stretcher out to the rear entrance and put in the ambulance. As Bill lay in there, he wondered if Marsh had managed to find out where Pat Harrison was staying tonight. He thought of Jane hearing the news and hoped she would call Marsh if she became anxious. Bill was aware that he couldn't ring her on his mobile as a strict security code was in force which forbade all but emergency calls. He thought what a danger policing had become since he joined the force as a young constable. He was remembering how when a policeman put his hand up for you to stop you stopped. There was a respect for the uniform in those days. Whereas now, if you stood in front of a speeding car signalling it to stop, it might run straight over you. Now here he was, bandaged as an injured copper and all to try and trap a villain named Bob Plummer. Bill even smiled to himself at the thought of the ludicrous situation he was in, lying in bed surrounded by armed police officers in white coats pretending to be nurses and doctors.

★　★　★

Sergeant Marsh had tried Pat Harrison's number twice but each time she was on voicemail so he left it until he could speak to her personally. It was while he was wondering how his inspector was getting on that he received a call from Bill's wife Jane, who wasn't her usual cheerful self.

'It's Jane Forward, Sergeant. I'm sorry to bother you but is my husband there?'

'No. He's out on a job at the moment. Is something the matter?'

'Well, I tried his mobile but it's only taking messages.'

She sounded anxious so he tried to put her mind at rest. 'Yes. The job he's on requires silence so mobile phones are restricted, I'm afraid.'

'Oh, I see. Only I was listening to the radio and heard that a senior police officer has been injured by a letter bomb and was in hospital. My husband had warned me to look out for any suspicious mail so I naturally wondered if it was something sent to him at the police station.'

'That's the job your husband has gone to but it's all a bit hush-hush at the moment. No doubt he will be phoning in once he knows all the facts. But he's perfectly all right, I promise you.' Marsh sounded convincing.

'Thank you. I shall hope to hear from him

when he's got a minute then,' she said.

'If I speak to him I shall tell him you called.'

'Thank you, Sergeant.'

Constable Ruth Cunningham raised an inquisitive eyebrow as Jane hung up. 'Well?' she asked.

'It wasn't my husband, thank goodness, but he's gone to the hospital to investigate what happened. That's why his mobile was switched off, I assume.'

'Yes, they don't like mobile phones in certain areas of hospitals. They interfere with their electronic equipment.' Although Jane appeared to accept that explanation, Ruth was not convinced and wished she knew what was really happening.

★　★　★

Pat Harrison had just left her first client of the day and was checking her voicemail to see if anyone had called. There was a message from Belling and Musgrove asking her to see another client that afternoon. She called them back to check the details.

'Hello, Bernard, it's Pat. I've just got your message.'

'This is a gentleman in apartment eleven, Grove Court, Paddington. His name is

Norman Morris and his Aunt Betty has left him £50,000. Because this is a last-minute job for you, I have checked the Albany Hotel quite near Paddington Station and they've got a room. I have asked them to reserve it for you until midday in case you have nowhere else in mind.'

'That will be fine, Bernard, it's a nice hotel. I've not stayed there but I had a meal there once.'

'OK, I'll ring and confirm it for you and I'll email the details to you straightaway so keep your laptop switched on.'

Pat got a taxi from Forest Hill to the Albany, Paddington. She had her laptop switched on, heard a bleep and went to her emails. The Albany had confirmed her reservation, so she could relax. She was about to go to her website for hotels in the Paddington area to see if she had ever stayed in one when the taxi came to a sudden stop to avoid a dog. Pat grabbed her laptop to prevent it falling to the floor and saw something that shocked her. It was describing the way to make a letter bomb. Somehow she had brought up the details but couldn't understand how they had got on to her laptop. She had never let anyone else use it and the only time it was out of her sight was when it was in her hotel room. Pat racked her brains and then remembered that the only time she had left it with someone else was when she left Bob alone in her room. Suddenly she was wondering if he had been lying to her all the time. She remembered him saying he had to find a policeman and see if he had been injured. And his excuse to keep changing the colour and style of his hair had sounded rather theatrical to her. She didn't know what to do. If she asked Bob, to satisfy her curiosity, he might turn nasty again and she was scared that he could become dangerous. And why would Bob Wilson want to make a letter bomb? And was Wilson his real name? Pat's mind was going round and round like a windmill and she wished she knew what to do. She decided that she would not tell Bob where she was staying tonight. Not until she had sorted this mystery out.

She arrived at the Albany and checked in. Her room was very comfortable but it was a single and only had a four foot wide single bed. She switched on the radio and got some music while she made notes from Bernard's email regarding her client. She was writing, 'Norman Morris, 11 Grove Court, had been left £50,000 from his Aunt Betty's will' when she suddenly heard the news item saying that a senior police officer had been injured by a letter bomb and taken to hospital. She froze for a moment then without hesitation dialled 999.

★ ★ ★

The lift stopped at the first floor of the hospital so that the people guarding Bill Forward could easily see anyone from his ward. There were several people coming and going all the time. Some were obviously visitors to other wards on that floor and others, who were injured, were stretching their legs. From his bed, Bill could see a man with a bandaged face and Bill was suddenly extremely grateful he had avoided the blast from the letter bomb. He knew he could have lost his sight if Bob Plummer had been successful. Lying there with only a small space between the bandages to see through, he wondered what made men like Plummer so evil while other criminals had a code of honour that he could respect. The man with the bandaged face had a stoop and Bill wondered what his injuries were. Feeling sorry for the man, he noticed him looking towards the people in Bill's ward. It was the way he squinted that made Bill suddenly suspicious and he gave Roberts a look that he quickly understood. Roberts stood close and listened to Bill.

'The man out there with a stoop and his face bandaged. See if he leaves with his face covered. I can't be sure but he could be Plummer,' Bill whispered.

'OK.'

Roberts, in his white coat, pretended to make Bill more comfortable then walked to the hall, passing closer to the man. As he stood behind him, Roberts looked for any sign of injury but could see nothing. He took a towel from a cupboard and walked back to Bill's bed. 'I can't see any sign of injury, sir, but with all that bandage it is hard to tell. I'll keep a close eye on him. Just try and relax.'

Bill looked back to the hall and saw the man walking quickly to the stairs. He gave Roberts instructions. 'If he goes to the car park and attempts to get in a car and drive, I want him arrested and brought here, understood?'

'Yes, sir.'

Roberts made his way to the stairs and followed the man down to the next floor and through a door leading to some first-floor wards. The man went into a ward and sat in the comfortable chair beside his bed. Roberts watched him sit, trying to regain his normal breathing rhythm. As he turned to leave, the ward sister approached him.

'He's quite a man, our Barry. He insists on climbing the stairs every day despite his problem,' she said.

'Yes, I've seen him up there. What's wrong with him?'

'He's lost much of his lower jaw and one lung due to a car crash. His son was driving but he didn't survive.'

'Poor man. Well, I had better get back to my ward,' said Roberts.

Bill Forward listened with interest to what Roberts had to tell him about the man with his face bandaged and began to wonder if Plummer would ever turn up.

★   ★   ★

DS Marsh was waiting in his office, hoping to hear that his Inspector was not lying in the hospital in vain, when he had a call from Superintendent Lamb.

'Get up to my office right away, Marsh. I've some good news at last.'

'I'm on my way, sir.'

Marsh hurried to hear the good news Lamb was talking about. He knocked at the door and went into his office.

'Now listen, Sergeant, and listen carefully. A 999 call was made a few moments ago from a Paddington hotel. The caller was a lady, a Miss Pat Harrison.'

'The woman Plummer stayed with in her

hotels! I was going to phone her office to try and find out where she was staying tonight.'

'Well, now you don't have to. You can get over to the Albany Hotel and talk to her face to face.'

'Is Plummer likely to be there tonight?' asked Marsh.

'According to Miss Harrison, she had no idea she was going to be there herself until a short while ago. And she has not been in touch with him since then, she said.'

Marsh was confused as he asked, 'Who was she telling all this to?'

'Me.' Lamb smiled. 'As soon as I heard that there had been a 999 regarding our letter bomb news item I wanted to know exactly what was going on. So now I want you to go to the Albany Hotel. Walker from armed protection will be there, just in case Plummer should turn up. Call in on DI Forward on the way and let him know what you're up to. He may have another idea he wants you to try while you chat to Pat Harrison.'

'He'll probably want to come with me, knowing him, sir.'

'Well, that is a definite no-no. Plummer might still go to the hospital, remember. We cannot afford to take chances.'

'I know.'

'And take those photographs of Plummer

with you. Miss Harrison can confirm what he is looking like now.'

'I keep them on me all the time now.'

'Good man. Off you go and keep in touch, Sergeant.'

'I will, sir.' Marsh left the office and went to the car park. He was looking forward to seeing his inspector and giving him the news about Pat Harrison and his forthcoming meeting with her. This was certainly the break they were hoping for and it seemed just a matter of time before they had Bob Plummer locked safely away. Marsh could only imagine what Bill had been going through and hoped the news he was going to give him would cheer him up. When he arrived at the hospital car park, it was full. There were cars waiting for a space and he didn't have time to queue. He parked in an area reserved for doctors only and managed to squeeze into a small space. He knew Bill was on the first floor and walked up the stairs. Recognizing two of the men dressed in white coats, he knew he was at the right ward and saw his inspector looking surprised to see him. Marsh went over to him and sat by his bed.

'What are you doing here?' asked Bill.

'I've got some good news,' he whispered.

'Are they kicking me out?' Bill said hopefully.

'Pat Harrison called 999 with news about

Plummer making a letter bomb. I'm going to see her now to get the full story. Baa-Baa wanted me to let you know and see how you want me to play it.'

'So here's a turn-up for the book. You were going to try and find out where she was staying so that we could pull Plummer into our trap and now she calls us to tell us he made a letter bomb! I think you will just have to use your police instinct with this, sunshine. Where are you meeting her?'

'I'm seeing her at the Albany Hotel, Paddington.'

'Is that where she was last night?'

'No. It's where she's staying tonight.'

'Well, you be careful in case this is one of Plummer's ideas and she's just being used to set us up.'

'Walker will be there if I need him,' said Marsh.

Bill looked anxious. 'Let's hope you don't.'

'I'd better get going or she might get suspicious of us.'

Marsh stood up and turned to leave when Bill said, 'Have you got the doctored photographs?'

'They're in my pocket.'

Marsh left the ward and Bill wished he was going with him. He just hoped Pat Harrison's 999 was a genuine call and that Marsh was not going to be in any danger.

16

Marsh arrived at the Albany Hotel to find Walker waiting for him. They approached the reception desk and Marsh gave the girl a smile.

'Put me through to Miss Harrison's room, please.'

The girl dialled the number and indicated that Marsh use the desk phone.

When her phone rang, Pat was apprehensive as she picked it up. 'Hello.'

'Miss Harrison?'

'Yes.'

'We've come in response to your telephone call. May we come up?'

'Yes. I'm in room six.' Pat was both nervous and relieved as she waited. She was frightened as to what Bob would do if he knew she had called the police. She had only seen his temper on that one occasion when she interrupted while he was listening for news of an injured police officer. But that had frightened her, and the only feeling of safety she had at the moment was the fact that Bob had no idea where she was staying. The knock at the door made her jump and she opened it to see Marsh holding his warrant card for her to see. 'Please come in,' she said. As the two men walked into her room, she looked up the corridor to make sure no-one else had seen them.

'I am DS Marsh and this is DC Walker and we want to talk to you about your 999 call and why you made it.'

Pat sat on the edge of the bed and said, 'I heard on the news that a police officer had been injured by a letter bomb and suddenly it all made sense.'

'What did?'

'Well, I had a gentleman friend staying with me who said he was a private investigator and was looking for a police officer who had been injured by a letter bomb. Then it all came back to me. He was alone in my room a couple of days earlier and must have used my laptop.'

'Used it for what?'

'On my way over here I was holding it on my lap because I was waiting for confirmation from my office that I had a room reserved here. The taxi pulled up sharply and I had to grab the laptop to stop it falling to the floor. Maybe it was the way I handled it, I don't know — anyway, I accidentally brought up a website saying 'How to make a letter bomb' and it all came back to me. I put two and two together and it scared me. That's when I dialled 999.'

'This gentleman you had staying with you, what was his name?' asked Marsh.

'Bob Wilson. He said he was a private investigator and had to find a policeman who had been injured.'

Marsh took the two photographs of Plummer from his pocket and showed them to her. 'Is this the man?'

Pat was surprised to see that the police had Bob's photographs after he had changed his appearance. 'Yes, that's him. That's Bob Wilson.'

Marsh took the photographs back. 'His name isn't Wilson, it's Plummer. He's wanted for beating up a police officer and of course making and sending a letter bomb to a senior police officer, with intent to cause serious injury. I'm afraid your gentleman friend is a violent, dangerous man and has to be caught and put away. And with your help he will be. Are you prepared to help us?'

The idea of getting further involved with Bob's capture made Pat very nervous. 'If he found out that I helped put him away, he'd kill me.'

'You will have twenty-four hour protection until he gets picked up and there's no need for him to ever know you were involved. But at the moment you are the one person that *can* help us. What do you say?'

Pat thought about the fantastic sex life she had known with Bob and then how he had lied to her about his work and used her laptop to make a letter bomb. 'What do you want me to do?'

'While I think of it, does he carry a gun?' asked Marsh.

She shook her head. 'No. If he had a gun he would have wanted to show it to me so as to impress me.'

'Well, the people protecting you will. They are like Walker here, all members of the armed protection unit, so you will be quite safe. And now I would like you to call Plummer and tell him where you are staying tonight.'

'Oh God, do I have to?'

'We have to let him think you want to see him,' said Marsh. 'He mustn't know what you found on the laptop. As far as he is concerned, your relationship is just the same. You would normally let him know which hotel you were going to be in, wouldn't you?'

'Yes.'

'So that's what you must do.'

Before she could do anything, her mobile rang. She looked at it nervously. 'Christ, it's Bob calling from his mobile!'

'Tell him you are with a client and will call him back in ten minutes,' said Marsh.

Pat tried to compose herself and answered the call. 'Hello, Bob. I'm with a client at the moment. I'll call you back in ten minutes.' She rang off and sat nervously, trying to pull herself together.

'So he's got a mobile,' said Marsh. 'Have you got the number?'

'Yes.' She wrote the number on the phone pad and gave it to Marsh. 'He only got it recently. Now I never know where he is.'

'Now that we have his number, with our modern technology we will always know where he is while his phone is switched on. When you call him back tell him you'll meet him in the bar because you only have a small single room.'

'Suppose he tries for a double room and they happen to have one from a cancellation. What do I do then?' said Pat.

'It doesn't matter as long as you get him to come out into the open because then we will have him.'

The next ten minutes passed slowly and Pat grew increasingly nervous about calling Bob. She did not want to sound anything but normal when she spoke to him and hoped she could pull it off. As the three of them waited in silence, she thought about the incredible nights she had experienced total satisfaction in sexual desire. Now all that would come to an end and Bob would spend the next few years locked up in prison.

Marsh checked his watch. 'You can call him now, Miss Harrison.'

'I'm not looking forward to this,' she said.

'Just relax and sound pleased to be speaking to him. And apologize for having to hang up on him.'

Pat took a few deep breaths then punched Bob's number into her mobile. He answered immediately.

'Hello, gorgeous, where are you?'

'I'm in a hotel in Paddington. Where are you?'

'Getting horny thinking of you in a lovely hotel, waiting for me to come and try your bed out.'

'Sorry I had to hang up on you when you called me, Bob. I had a client with me.'

'So you said. I hope he wasn't trying your bed out.'

'Don't be silly. As a matter of fact I've only got a single room here. There's no room to swing a cat round. I tried for a double but this was all they had.'

'Are you saying I won't see you tonight?'

Her mouth began to dry. 'Of course I'll see you tonight. I thought we could meet in the bar here, have a drink and find somewhere else to stay.'

There was something about her voice that made him feel uneasy. This wasn't the Pat he knew. She wasn't giving him her usual sexy replies. 'Where is your hotel?'

'It's the Albany.' She looked at a note Marsh passed to her and read what he had written. 'Jump in a taxi and come over. I'll see you in the bar.'

Bob had an uncomfortable feeling she was not alone and became nervous. 'OK, I'll be there soon.' As soon as he rang off, he got the number for the Albany and called it.

'Hello, I believe you have a Miss Harrison staying with you.'

'Yes, we do, sir.'

'Is she alone? I don't want to disturb her if she isn't.'

'I think the gentlemen are still with her, sir.'

'Oh, they're still there, that's good.'

'Do you want me to tell her you called, sir?'

'No, I'll catch up with her later.'

Bob rang off. Now he knew his suspicions were right. She was with someone and he had a horrible feeling it could be the law. Why else would Pat get so nervous? One thing Bob would not be doing today was going to the Albany Hotel.

★ ★ ★

Marsh and Walker were in the bar waiting for Plummer to turn up. Pat Harrison was sitting alone at a table drinking a gin and tonic and watching nervously for Bob. There were several people in the bar and she hoped she could face him without looking the way she felt, nervous. After almost forty-five minutes had passed, Marsh walked over to her table and asked her to phone Bob and see how long he might be. Marsh got his ear as close as he could to her mobile so that he could hear what Bob said. She called his number and they heard him say hello.

'Hello, Bob. I'm waiting in the bar. How long will you be?'

'Missing me, are you?'

'Of course I am.'

'Surely you aren't lonely? Not with your gentlemen friends there.'

His remark threw Pat offguard for a moment. 'Who are you talking about? What gentlemen friends?'

'The ones you had in your room with you earlier.'

'One was a client and the other man was his secretary. He was there to make sure the client understood the facts of his legacy.' Pat hoped she sounded convincing. 'Who did you think they were?'

Bob waited a moment before answering. 'I

don't know and that's the trouble, Pat. I don't know you any more.'

'What do you mean?'

'I mean I don't trust you, Pat. I can tell by your voice that you've changed. You're keeping something from me and it worries me. So I won't be seeing you any more.' He rang off.

Pat was surprised at Bob's reaction and gave Marsh a despondent shrug. 'I'm sorry.'

'Don't be. You were fine. He's got the mind of a guilty man, that's why he behaved like he did.' Marsh moved over to Walker with Plummer's mobile number. 'Get our people to put a track on this. I want to know where he is and where he's going all the time his mobile is on. Tell them to report to me or DI Forward.'

'I'll do it from the car,' said Walker.

As Walker left the bar, Marsh realized that Pat would have to move out of the hotel in case Plummer came back to look for her. 'Where will you go now, Miss Harrison?'

'I've got to meet a client and tell him an aunt has left him a large legacy, then I shall go home.'

'Does Plummer know where you live?'

She thought for a moment. 'Now that you mention it, no, he never asked. Come to think of it, I don't know where he lives either.

Although he gave me the impression he had a place in Soho, or that might have been a hotel that's had to close. He lied so convincingly I don't know what's true and what isn't.'

'It doesn't matter. We can get you police protection until he is safely locked up.' Marsh gave her his notebook. 'Write your address there, please.' He waited for her to finish then saw that it was an apartment. 'Do you live alone?'

'Yes.'

'Could someone else stay with you?'

'There's a single guest room.'

'So you could have twenty-four-hour protection. I would like to arrange that. She will be a trained police officer, in the event that Bob Plummer turns up. Meanwhile, Walker will stay with you and see you safely home.'

'This policewoman won't be in uniform, will she?'

Marsh smiled. 'No, she will be in ordinary clothing. Your neighbours won't know she's a policewoman, if that's what's bothering you — just a friend who is staying with you.'

Pat was relieved. 'Oh, that's good.'

Walker came back and gave Marsh the thumbs-up. Marsh told him what he wanted him to do and headed back to see Bill in the hospital. On the way he made arrangements for an armed protection policewoman to stay with Pat Harrison.

★ ★ ★

Bob Plummer was running short of money and called Steve Saunders on his mobile.

'Hello, Steve, it's me, Bob.'

'Yes, I can hear that. So you've got your own mobile now.'

'I thought I needed one, so I bought one from the money we made together. Like you said, we're a good team, so why don't we make some more?'

'I had no way to contact you — I was going to suggest the same thing. But now that you've got a mobile and I can get hold of you, let's put our skills to the test again,' said Steve with enthusiasm. 'Let's meet and have a drink, eh?'

'Good idea. When do you suggest?'

'What are you doing now?'

'Nothing special, I'm just wandering down Regent Street at the moment.'

'Let's meet at the Greek bar at the back of the old Café Royal. I can be there in fifteen minutes and it's easy for me to park there.'

'OK.'

'See you soon, Bob.'

Plummer was pleased to think he would be

making some money again and hoped he could find a place that was more permanent where he could get his head down for a while. Before he met Steve, he wanted to know for sure that his letter bomb had really done what he hoped it had. He telephoned the Chelsea police station and got through to their enquiry desk.

'Hello, I wonder if you can help me. I'm an old colleague of DI Forward and have just heard that he has been in an incident with an explosive device. Is this true and is he badly hurt, do you know?'

'I can only tell you that he is in Chelsea and Westminster hospital at the moment, sir. As to his condition, only staff at the hospital can tell you that but I understand his face and hands suffered injury.'

'Thank you. I shall contact the hospital as you suggest.' Bob rang off, feeling happy with the information. He decided he would celebrate with a large drink at the Greek bar when Steve arrived.

★   ★   ★

Marsh was just pulling up to park at the hospital when his phone rang.

'DS Marsh.'

'It's Peterson here, Sergeant. We've got Bob

Plummer's mobile on track and he's going down Regent Street from Oxford Circus, heading south towards Piccadilly Circus.'

'Let me know if he stops anywhere.'

'I will as long as he leaves his mobile on. Once he turns it off we won't know where he is until we can use the tracker again.'

'Fingers crossed he leaves it on, then we can get some of our lads to pick him up. Keep me informed.'

'I will.'

Marsh parked and went up to the first-floor ward to see Bill Forward. As he was lying in bed, the dressing round his face and hands looked very convincing. He was obviously pleased to see Marsh.

'Well, Marsh, I hope you're the bringer of good news?'

'We have a track on Plummer and he's walking down Regent Street in the direction of Piccadilly Circus. If he stops somewhere and leaves his mobile on, we can nab him.'

'That's what I like to hear. I'll get two plain clothes men from armed protection there. They've got his photograph so he should be easy to spot. And you get there as well. I shall give the super a ring and tell him what we're doing. He said to keep him informed so let's hope this pleases him.'

★   ★   ★

When Bob Plummer arrived at the Greek bar
it was busy but not full. He ordered himself
a large whisky and sat at a table. There was a
sign requesting that mobile phones be used
outside the bar unless in an emergency. Bob
switched his phone off and enjoyed his
whisky. He thought of the money he could
make with Steve and wondered if he would
ever meet a girl like Pat again. It was his one
regret, that this incredible lover had looked
like becoming a danger to him, and he
wondered why. If there had been a reward out
for him it would explain her change of mood
but as far as he knew there wasn't. As he
looked out of the window, he saw Steve's car
pull up and park. When Steve walked in, Bob
had almost finished his drink.

'Hello, Bob. I see you're nearly finished so
let me get you a fresh one. What is it?'

'A large whisky please, Steve.'

'That's just what I fancy but I have to be
careful when I'm driving.' He ordered the
drinks and took them to the table. 'I was
pleased you've got yourself a mobile. Now
we can keep in touch on a regular basis. We'll
make a lot of money, Bob.'

Bob smiled. 'Those words are music to my
ears. Cheers.' He picked up his fresh whisky

247

and enjoyed taking a large swig.

'Cheers,' said Steve and picked up his pint of lager.

'So what have you got in mind?' Bob asked him.

'Well, I thought we could go back to Luke Street where we had our first lucky day. There are no cameras round there and a lot of people use the machines in that area. We can't use this area. They've got more cameras than a railway station around here.'

'I'm happy to give Luke Street another go,' Bob told him. 'When do you want to do it?'

'What about tomorrow morning?'

'What time?'

'Ten o'clock?'

'Great.' Bob drank his whisky right down to the bottom of the glass. 'I think I shall have one more before I find a place to stay tonight. After all, I'm not driving.' He grinned.

'I thought you'd be staying with your lady-friend.'

'Yeah, so did I but that came to a sudden end, I'm afraid.'

'Why, what happened?'

'She got involved with some other men, so I shan't be seeing her again.'

'So now you're looking for a place?'

'Just for tonight. Once we get some money

tomorrow I can find a place more permanent for a while.'

'Well, we can put you up for tonight.'

'Are you sure?'

'Of course I am. Then we can take a bottle back with us and have a nice drink at home.'

'Your wife won't mind me coming back?'

'Don't worry. She's got a skirt but I wear the trousers.'

Steve finished his drink and they left the bar and went to his car. Bob sat in the passenger seat, feeling happy to have got a free room for the night. As the car pulled out into Regent Street, Bob noticed two men looking up and down the area as if searching for someone in particular. His instinct made him duck down to keep his face from view. The traffic was busy and the car was almost at a standstill.

'What's the matter, Bob?'

'I just saw someone I don't want to see just now so I'll keep my head down till we get moving.'

'It's the lights holding us up but they're changing now so we'll be off again.' Steve drove away. 'You can get up now.'

Bob sat up again and tried to think of an excuse for his action. 'Sorry about that. It was a man I try to avoid if I can. I lent him some money once because he told me a sob story about him being out of work and his landlord saying he wanted his rent in advance or he would throw him out. It was all bullshit, of course, but I fell for it and now he's just a pain in the arse.'

'No wonder you wanted to avoid him.'

Bob had a natural ability to lie and was pleased Steve didn't know that the men were probably plain clothes policemen who were looking for Bob Plummer.

★ ★ ★

Marsh received a call from one of the policemen. 'No sign of him here, Sergeant. He may have gone down the stairs to the underground station.'

'In that case we'll never find him. If only he had left his mobile on for a few more minutes. Anyway, keep looking while I get back to DI Forward and let him know what's going on,' said Marsh.

When Bill Forward heard how close his men may have been to picking up Bob Plummer, he couldn't hide his frustration. 'Damn the man! He's like a cat with nine lives.'

'But one day soon he's going to run out of lives,' said Marsh.

'Well, I want to be there when he does. Not

lying here wrapped up like an Egyptian mummy. I'll have a word with the super and try and get clearance to come out of here.'

'Hold on a minute. If you're seen up and about without any injuries, Plummer will know his letter bomb didn't work and he might try something else. And that something *might* work. He's looking for vengeance and a man with his twisted mind could throw caution to the wind and succeed, but that wouldn't do *you* any good if you were killed.'

There was a moment's silence before Bill reluctantly had to agree. 'I always knew you would be a good copper one day, Marsh, and you're right, of course. If only we knew where the bastard was.'

⋆　⋆　⋆

They were halfway up Regent Street when Steve had to pull over to one side and allow an ambulance to get by. There was an unmarked police car in front of the Jaguar and Steve automatically flashed his lights to warn the driver that he also needed to pull over. The driver looked in his mirror and saw Bob Plummer in the car behind. Slowing right up, he was convinced he recognized the man in the passenger seat and said to his colleague, 'Don't turn round but there's a photo on the board back at the nick of a man they want for GBH at Chelsea. Call in and tell Chelsea he's in a white Jaguar just behind us. Do they want us to pull him in or have they got their own men tailing him?'

Because the car in front was going slower than it needed to, Bob sensed something was wrong and became nervous. Sitting with his hand up to his face he said, 'What is that berk in front doing? Can't we get past him?'

'I was just about to,' said Steve. 'Hang on.' He swung out of the line and was quickly away.

A large van overtook the unmarked police car, making it impossible for anything else to pass it. By the time the police had a clear view of the road ahead, they had lost sight of the Jaguar.

★   ★   ★

'But surely they got the Jaguar's number!' said Bill, when he heard what had happened.

'Apparently it was too close for them to see at first. Then a van blocked their view. It was definitely W19, something, and the last letters were either ULA or OLA But with the W reg we know it's a 2000 model.'

'I don't believe it. There must be hundreds of white Jags that were registered in 2000. At this rate they'll still be looking for Plummer after I've retired! It's no good, Marsh. It might be a risk but I've got to get out of here. I want to spend tonight in my own bed and without the bandages. I'm going to call Lamb.' He rang off before Marsh could talk him out of it.

Lamb listened to Bill's reasoning. 'I can understand how you feel but if you come out into the open after all we have done to protect you, and Plummer knows you weren't even scratched by his letter bomb, he isn't going to give up.'

'I am aware of that, sir, but there is something I've just thought of. One thing that might give us a lead as to where he is and who he's with.'

'What's that, Forward?'

'Well, we normally have to go to our vehicle records people to find out who the registered keeper of a vehicle is and they look it up on their computer, don't they?'

'That's the normal procedure, yes.'

'Well, I know that Chief Superintendent Bradley is a friend of the officer in charge over there and wondered if he could twist his arm to do us a big favour.'

'What sort of big favour?'

'Get a list of all the W registration white Jaguars with any of the other numbers or letters the lads in the unmarked car saw and send them through to us so that I can scan through them. I might spot a name that rings a bell. Our friend Bob Plummer must be chummy with the white Jag owner and it could be just the break we're looking for.'

'It's unlikely he'll agree but I'll see what Mr Bradley says and get back to you.'

Bill waited impatiently to hear the decision. Finally, after ten minutes had passed, the call came through.

'You will be pleased to hear that because of the danger Plummer threatens, your request to have a list of the W reg white Jag owners put through to us has been agreed. I'll get you out of there and back here just as soon as I can. But keep the bandages on until you are here just in case Plummer or one of his pals should see you.'

Bill was happy to be going back to Chelsea police station and was keeping his fingers crossed that he would find a connection between the white Jag, its owner and Plummer. He called Marsh and told him he would see him back at the office.

* * *

Steve Saunders showed Bob the single bedroom. It was a clean room with a single bed, small wardrobe and a chest of drawers and Bob was grateful to have somewhere to stay. Steve's wife had offered to cook a dinner for them and as he wouldn't have to drive, Steve was prepared to start drinking. The two men finished what was left of the whisky in one bottle and opened a fresh one.

'This is the life, Steve. I envy you.'

'You do?'

'Of course I do. You've got your own home and a woman to take care of you. What more could a man want? Apart from money, I mean.'

'Yeah, Eileen's all right. She looks after me, as you say, but I thought you had a nice lady to shack up with.'

'So did I.' Bob sighed. 'But she turned out to be a dark horse. She had other men calling on her behind my back and I got the feeling she was ready to turn me over to the police. I couldn't trust her, Steve. If I had I might have ended up inside again, so she had to go, I'm afraid.'

'In those circumstances I don't blame you. But now you're a free man again you can do what you like, Bob. You'll soon find another woman. Especially when we do a few cash machines and you're in the money again.'

'But no-one as good as Pat in bed. She was something special.'

Bob sat thinking about Pat and wondered why there was now only one person in the world he could trust — and that was Steve Saunders, a man he had met in prison.

★   ★   ★

Bill Forward arrived back at his office and was happy to be sitting at his desk again. Now free of his bandages, he felt like a human being once more and was waiting for a call to tell him the computer room had the information he wanted.

Marsh arrived a few minutes later and greeted him with a handshake. 'Nice to see you back, sir.'

'It's nice to *be* back, Sergeant. I'm just waiting for the info to arrive, then I can go and look at the computer and hope I find what I'm looking for.'

'How did you manage to swing them sending it to you?'

Bill lowered his voice to a secretive tone. 'Just between you and me, Marsh, the chief super is an old friend of mine. Do anything for me he will.' Marsh responded with a look of incredulity but before he could say anything Bill's phone rang to tell him the information he was waiting for had arrived. 'It's come through. Wish me luck, sunshine.'

He got out of the office and hurried to the computer room.

After a while, Superintendent Lamb put his head round the door and saw Bill looking carefully at the list on the computer in front of him. 'How are you doing, Forward?'

'There are more here than I had bargained for so it may take a while to find a match.'

'Well, you carry on and let me know the minute you find something.'

'I will, sir.'

Lamb had only been gone a few minutes when it came up on the screen: W192 ULA. Keeper Stephen Saunders, 87 Brunnel Street, Tottenham. Bill was excited as he wrote down the details. His hunch had paid off and he went straight to Lamb's office.

'I've got it, sir, it just came through.'

'Who is the registered keeper?'

'It's a Stephen Saunders, he lives in Tottenham.'

'So there's a chance Plummer is still with him and you no doubt want to surprise him if he is.'

'Can you imagine his face if I turned up to nick him?' Bill smiled.

'But if you turned up and Plummer *isn't* with him? All you will have achieved is to let him know you were not hurt by his letter bomb and we'll be back to square one again.'

Bill was reluctant to agree but knew Lamb was right. 'I shall put the place under surveillance and make sure he *is* there before any move is made to arrest him.'

'Let our surveillance chaps arrest Plummer if he's there.'

'But surely I've earned the right to bring him in, sir?'

'You can have the pleasure of locking him up when he arrives here. I know you would personally like to arrest him after all he's put you and your wife through. But when he sees you shutting him in a cell, obviously unmarked by his letter bomb, he'll carry that memory with him for the rest of his days in prison.'

'Yes, I suppose you're right.'

'You know I am. Go and arrange the surveillance. I shall let Mr Bradley know you were right about tracing the white Jaguar.'

'Please thank the chief super for me.'

Bill went back to his office and joined Marsh.

'Any luck?' asked Marsh.

Bill took the paper with Saunders' name and address on and passed it to him. 'I was right, sunshine. This is where the Jag is so I want twenty-four-hour surveillance on this address. If there's any sign of Plummer I want to know. If he goes out I want him followed and if our lads have to arrest him they must put the cuffs on him. I don't want him disappearing again. While you are doing that I'm going to follow up another hunch of mine.' He rang the prison where Bob Plummer had served his five years and spoke to the governor. 'This is DI Forward, Chelsea police sir, I wonder if you can help me.'

'I will if I can, Inspector.'

'When you had Bob Plummer there, was a prisoner by the name of Stephen Saunders with you during that time?'

The governor was thoughtful for a moment. 'Saunders . . . Saunders . . . Yes, he was a pickpocket doing six months. He and Plummer became quite friendly as I recall.'

'That's what I wanted to know. Thank you, sir, you've been a great help.' Bill was pleased his call had not been in vain. He rang off and waited for Marsh to finish his call.

'They're putting two men on twenty-four-hour surveillance at Saunders' address. They will report directly to you if, and when, Plummer shows his face,' Marsh told him.

'Good. My hunch was right by the way. Plummer and Saunders were in prison together and became friendly. Saunders was a dip doing six months,' said Bill.

'What do you think Plummer will get this time?'

'A damn sight more than the five years he got for beating his wife. He beat up Dave Lockhart, the other policeman with me when we made the arrest. Then he tried to injure me with a homemade letter bomb. My guess is a judge will put him away for a very long time.'

★   ★   ★

The sky was getting dark and there was lightning in the distance as Steve looked out of his living-room window. 'It looks like we're in for a storm.'

Bob had drunk a lot of whisky and was unsteady on his feet as he went to the window. 'Looks like the middle of the night out there. What time is it anyway?' He stood peering at his watch, trying to get it into focus.

'It's ten past nine,' said Steve.

'Time we had another drink then.' Bob grinned.

Neither of them had noticed the car that was parked a little further up on the opposite side of the road. The driver put a call through to Bill Forward.

'It's Sergeant Lucas here, sir. PC Malcolm and I are here, almost outside 87 Brunnel Street and your man Plummer *is* there. He and another man just came to the window and looked out.'

'Did they see you?'

'No, sir. I think they were more interested in a thunderstorm that's heading this way.'

'Right, arrest Plummer and bring him in.'

'What about the other man?'

'Charge him with aiding and abetting a known criminal. I don't think you will have any trouble with *him*. He's a dip Plummer got friendly with in prison, not a violent man. But make sure you cuff Plummer's hands behind his back. You don't want him able to bring his hands up and over your head. If he did his cufflinks would choke you to death.'

'I understand, sir. We'll go over now, read them their rights and bring them in.'

Bill rang off, keeping his fingers crossed that nothing would go wrong.

★　★　★

When they arrived at the police station, the last person Bob Plummer expected to see was Bill Forward. His shock was something he couldn't hide and his voice trembled when he said, 'You're not injured at all!'

Bill took a firm grip on his arm and walked him to the custody suite. 'No, Mr Plummer. You tried to fool us with your beard and dyed hair, but now you've been the victim of *our* deception.' The custody sergeant charged Plummer with sending a letter bomb to Inspector Forward with intent to cause serious injury. He then made Plummer empty his pockets, the contents of which were listed and put into a plastic bag. He was then informed that he would appear before the court tomorrow. Bill took Plummer away and stopped at a cell door. He guided him in and with a feeling of satisfaction, closed the steel door and locked it. The man who had threatened vengeance was now locked up and wondering how many years the court would sentence him to. He sat looking at the door and said in a quiet, but threatening voice, 'One day I'll have you, Forward. No matter how long it takes, I'll have you. And that's a promise!'

Epilogue

Steve Saunders was charged with harbouring a wanted man but as he wasn't involved in Plummer's past or his attempt to injure a police officer, he was released on police bail.

Sergeant Marsh called Pat Harrison and told her of Bob Plummer's arrest and that her policewoman minder would now return to other duties. Pat looked forward to having her privacy again. She had left Belling and Musgrove and changed her mobile phone number so that Bob wouldn't be able to find her. Although she missed her nights with him, she was not short of male company for very long.

★   ★   ★

Bill Forward was relaxing at home. It was one of those weekends when things were back to normal. Jane had cooked the Sunday roast while Bill sat reading the paper. He had heard from Father O'Connor that Ronnie Hicks had been released from the clinic and was perfectly fit again. Bill was pleased Dave Norris had got Hicks into the clinic and that the treatment to clear his body of drugs had been successful. Bob Plummer had received a fifteen-year prison sentence for the beating he gave Lockhart, and his intent to cause serious injury with a letter bomb. But Bill Forward knew that Plummer could still be a threat to him when he had served his time and was released.

Then, out of the blue, he received news from Superintendent Lamb that Plummer would not be able to carry out his threat of vengeance. After only three weeks in prison, he had suffered a massive heart attack from which he never recovered.

We do hope that you have enjoyed reading this large print book.

Did you know that all of our titles are available for purchase?

We publish a wide range of high quality large print books including:
Romances, Mysteries, Classics
General Fiction
Non Fiction and Westerns

Special interest titles available in large print are:
The Little Oxford Dictionary
Music Book
Song Book
Hymn Book
Service Book

Also available from us courtesy of Oxford University Press:
Young Readers' Dictionary
(large print edition)
Young Readers' Thesaurus
(large print edition)

For further information or a free brochure, please contact us at:
Ulverscroft Large Print Books Ltd.,
The Green, Bradgate Road, Anstey,
Leicester, LE7 7FU, England.
Tel: (00 44) **0116 236 4325**
Fax: (00 44) **0116 234 0205**

Other titles published by
The House of Ulverscroft:

A GAME OF MURDER

Ray Alan

Guests arrive at Stafford House for a Saturday evening buffet followed by party games, which include a game of murder. But they are unaware that a real murder has been planned, and that in turn is followed by a second death. Detective Inspector Bill Forward arrives to find there are eighteen suspects at the scene. Only after much patient investigation and strange leads can he bring the case to a surprising, unexpected conclusion.